"So, we've established that we both need money," he said. "How can I help with that?"

"I might have a solution for both of us to get the money we need."

"Tell me," he said in a reluctant tone, unsure if he actually wanted to hear what would come out of her mouth next.

She met his eyes and swallowed a couple of times. "To get the money...I need to be married."

Alarm bells clanged along with his radar and every hair on his body rose to attention.

Oh, hell no. Do not say what I think you are about to say.

"Would you consider..." She let out a quick breath.

Jake gripped the rock next to him hard enough to press painfully into his palm. *No! Don't ruin this by saying it.*

"This is a bigger ask than yours. Would you consider a marriage of convenience?" she said quickly and bit her lip again.

Jake was rarely speechless, but he was now. Bigger? Hell, this favor was enormous.

Dear Reader,

Welcome back to Oak Hollow, Texas! *A Marriage of Benefits* is the fourth book in my Home to Oak Hollow series, and I'm already working on books five and six. While writing this story, I got to live vicariously through the heroine as she works with animals. Some of the scenes are inspired by the raccoons who play on my back porch each night.

Jessica Talbot has left Hollywood for small-town Texas and plans to open a wildlife rescue in Oak Hollow, but the money she'd counted on is unavailable...unless she's married. When his teenage crush returns to Officer Jake Carter's life, she causes him one problem after another, and her offer of a marriage of convenience is a disaster waiting to happen. But...it could also be the answer to his problems. Even after several embarrassing encounters, will Jake Carter accept her offer?

I hope you enjoy *A Marriage of Benefits*, and if you haven't already, will check out the first three books in the series. I love connecting with readers, and you can visit me at makennalee.com. As always, thank you so much for reading.

Best wishes!

Makenna Lee

A Marriage of Benefits

MAKENNA LEE

HARLEQUIN
SPECIAL
EDITION

HARLEQUIN®

SPECIAL EDITION™

Recycling programs
for this product may
not exist in your area.

ISBN-13: 978-1-335-40844-0

A Marriage of Benefits

This edition published by arrangement with Harlequin Books S.A.

For questions and comments about the quality of this book, please contact us at CustomerService@Harlequin.com.

Harlequin Enterprises ULC
22 Adelaide St. West, 41st Floor
Toronto, Ontario M5H 4E3, Canada
www.Harlequin.com

Printed in U.S.A.

Makenna Lee is an award-winning romance author living in the Texas Hill Country with her real-life hero and their two children. Her writing journey began when she mentioned all her story ideas and her husband asked why she wasn't writing them down. The next day she bought a laptop, started her first book and knew she'd found her passion. Makenna is often drinking coffee while writing, reading or plotting a new story. Her wish is to write books that touch your heart, making you feel, think and dream.

Books by Makenna Lee

Harlequin Special Edition

Home to Oak Hollow

The Sheriff's Star
In the Key of Family
A Child's Christmas Wish

Visit the Author Profile page
at Harlequin.com for more titles.

To my book and wine club.
Thank you for all the laughs, advice and support.

Chapter One

"Ten miles to your destination," announced the monotone GPS voice.

Warm spring wind whipped strands of hair from Jessica Talbot's long braid, and the earthy scent of rain-dampened soil and sweet aroma of wildflowers evoked memories of her teenage summers spent in Oak Hollow.

"Oliver, you are going to love our new home. You'll have so much room to chase squirrels and sleep in the sun."

The big orange cat meowed and rubbed his head against the door of his carrier.

"I know you don't like being in there, Ollie, but it keeps you safe. It won't be long until you can get out."

Over the next hill she took in the view and released a long slow breath through a wide smile. The tree-lined road was flanked with a river of bluebonnets, a sprinkle of red and yellow flowers mixed in like colored stones. In the distance, the Welcome to Oak Hollow sign marked the finish line of her marathon from Hollywood. Old memories waited to be intertwined with new experiences, and once she crossed into the city limits, she'd start a new chapter with so much to look forward to.

Jessica still couldn't believe she owned the Williams ranch. She had wanted the one-hundred-acre paradise ever since the first summer vacation there with her father. When it had gone on the market, she hadn't thought twice about making an offer, even though it was above her price range by way more than a little bit. She'd now need to dip deeper than usual into her trust fund to open her veterinary practice. But moving to the Texas Hill Country was worth it.

"Ollie, I have a feeling we've left all of our bad luck behind. Apartment floods, scheming coworkers and all the Tinsel Town hustle and bustle."

The words had no sooner left her lips when her front right tire blew out, with a chorus of banging, flapping and her pulse keeping a rapid beat against her eardrums. The steering wheel jerked in her hands, making her swerve. She hit gravel along the road's edge and came to a shuddering stop with her heart in her throat.

"For the love of burned toast." She rested her forehead on the steering wheel and waited for her heart rate to normalize. "I should have known better than to say that aloud."

She rolled down all the windows for Oliver, climbed out to assess the damage and put an extra bit of force into slamming the door. She was thankful she'd checked her spare tire and replenished the must-carry essentials her father had always insisted on, especially before starting on a long journey.

Changing a tire had not been on today's schedule, but there would be no using a can of Fix-a-Flat for this mangled bit of rubber. It had probably been twelve years since her father had taught her to do this job, but his voice played clearly in her head, going through the steps of roadside tire changes in excruciating detail. More than once during this drive, she'd teared up when something reminded her of her father. This area of the country had been his favorite, and she missed him more than ever.

After getting out the jack, tire iron and spare, she worked up a sweat while loosening the tight lug nuts. Needing to apply extra muscle to get the tire off ended up landing her on her backside. And if that wasn't enough, she tore a hole in the knee of her blue jeans. With a few colorful phrases she'd never say in front of anyone, the tire was changed, and she was lowering the jack when the roar of an engine interrupted the birdsong. A black-and-white truck came over the hill in front of her and then pulled to a stop on the opposite shoulder of the road. Apparently, the local police drove big trucks with empty horse trailers.

She was still on her knees beside the front tire when an officer crossed the road. The sun was in her eyes as he approached, and she couldn't see his face until impressively broad shoulders blocked out the late-afternoon sun.

And what a wonderful face it was.

He lifted mirrored sunglasses to rest on his rich brown hair, revealing eyes the color of the ocean. His lips curved into a friendly smile.

A familiar smile. Her belly did a quick backflip.

"Would you like some help with that?" he asked.

His voice was another clue, and a glance at the nameplate on his breast pocket confirmed it. Her teenage crush, Jake Carter, was all grown up. The cute boy who had barely known she existed had become a very handsome adult.

"Ma'am, are you okay?" One of his eyebrows arched as his assessing gaze swept over her.

He doesn't recognize me. "Yes. Yes, I'm fine. Thanks for the offer, but I just finished and was about to put everything away."

Why did she have to be windblown, makeup free and wearing a baggy T-shirt with tire grease and half of her morning coffee decorating the front like abstract art? Jessica picked up the tools and headed for the back of her SUV, hoping he'd leave before he remembered her. If only she had a magic rewind button, she'd go all the way back to this morning when she should've put on her makeup. Mascara at the very least.

He followed her with the blown-out tire and put

it where she indicated beside a stack of boxes. "Are you just passing through?"

"I'm actually your newest resident." Metal clanged as she put the jack into its compartment. "I'm moving into my new house today."

He glanced at the two suitcases, sleeping bags and four boxes. "Traveling light?"

"The moving truck arrives tomorrow with the rest of my stuff."

His radio beeped. "Betty to 25," a woman's voice said in a jovial tone.

He pulled it from his belt. "Go for 25."

"Doc Ty will be ready for you when you get there with the horses."

"Ten-four. Thanks, Betty," he replied, then focused on Jessica. "If you're okay, I should get going."

"I'm fine. You go—" Her foot caught on something hidden in the thick grass and flowers along the roadside. As if in slow motion, she pitched forward and grabbed his shirtsleeve with enough force to yank him off balance. In an almost choreographed move, they spun until her back was headed for the ground. He slowed her fall enough that she landed softly in the carpet of bluebonnets with him braced above her, one hand cradling the back of her head.

Their gazes caught and held, but so briefly she couldn't read his mood. Her jolt of surprise gave way to embarrassment that swept over her in a wave of prickly heat. "I am so-o-o sorry," Jessica said once she had enough air in her lungs. "I'm such a klutz."

His friendly smile had disappeared, but he looked more confused than upset. "Are you hurt?"

"Only my pride." She tried to laugh but it came out as more of a whimper.

He had them both on their feet in seconds and frowned at the greasy handprint on his light blue uniform shirt before shifting his curious gaze back to her. "Have you been here before?"

"Yes, I'm..." If she withheld her name, maybe she could continue to be anonymous for a little while longer. Or forever. "I've been here a few times." It wasn't the ideal moment for a reunion with her old crush. Not when she looked a fright and had just stained his shirt. "Thanks for stopping to help. I'll be happy to pay for your dry cleaning." Spotting his sunglasses on the ground, Jessica picked them up and held them out, a new wave of heat flushing her face. "And if these are damaged, I'll buy you a new pair."

He took his sunglasses and gave them a quick inspection. "No need." There was more chatter on his radio. "Sorry. I need to get going."

"Of course. Hope the rest of your day is better than what I've just done to you."

His mouth kicked up into a grin. "I've had worse. Welcome to Oak Hollow. There's a tire shop on Fourth Street," he called over his shoulder as he jogged across the road.

Jessica climbed onto the driver's seat, caught her reflection in the rearview mirror and winced. It was worse than she'd thought. There was even a smudge of grease on her cheek from ear to chin. In a rush to leave this disaster scene behind, she kept her eyes focused straight ahead to avoid any risk of catching him laughing.

"Why was I too lazy to put on cute clothes today? I never do that." But she knew the answer. When she'd started her drive at four o'clock in the morning, comfort had been her only concern.

Her appearance didn't matter, or rather it shouldn't. All her focus needed to be on starting her veterinary practice, not looking for romance or thinking about a guy, even if he was the grown-up and very handsome version of her teen crush. Especially since one of her "rules for love" was never fall for a guy with a dangerous career. Her father's death had taught that painful lesson. And she could not forget that love had led her to bad choices and cost her a great job. A mistake she would not repeat.

She once again headed toward the city limits sign with Jake in her rearview mirror. She couldn't avoid him forever, but from now on, she would be sure to take time to look presentable before going out in public.

"Way to make an impression he'll never forget."

Jake Carter pulled a wet wipe from the truck's console and attempted to clean the grime from his sleeve, but he was only making it worse. Then he noticed the mud on his knees and groaned. "Great. Good thing the day is almost over."

There was a reason the guys teased him with the nickname Mr. Clean. But in his eyes, there was nothing wrong with a man wanting to have clean clothes and neat hair. His mother had taught him that your appearance told the world who you were and what you wanted them to think of you.

When he looked up, she had driven away. He wasn't sure what to make of Oak Hollow's newest resident. He hadn't even asked her name or introduced himself. Something about the woman—who his mom would call a hot mess—had thrown him off. If she'd been walking along the road, he would've thought she was a hitchhiker or accident victim in need of rescue. But even with her disheveled appearance, a sense of familiarity tugged on his mind. The spark of a memory he couldn't quite grasp. Who was this mystery woman? He'd no doubt see her around and could solve that mystery easily enough.

He pulled the department's truck and trailer up to the Smith farm where the word *Sold* had been posted across the top of the for-sale sign. The place had been freshened up with a new coat of white paint on the farmhouse and colorful flowers lining the front porch and walkway. Mrs. Smith stood at the fence feeding carrots to three horses. One was chestnut brown, one white and the third horse had a shiny black coat that glistened in the sunshine.

"How are you today, Mrs. Smith?"

"I'm very well." She pulled a carrot from the pocket of her purple overalls and handed it to Jake like he was still the little boy who liked to feed and ride her horses. "Before I forget, my neighbor Effie asked me to tell you her granddaughter is moving to town in a few weeks. She's very pretty, about your age and single."

Not another person trying to set me up.

"Is that right?" The town matchmakers had him on their radar, and like it or not, he was their current—and very reluctant—target. He didn't even bother to say that he wasn't staying in Oak Hollow. Even though he loved his hometown, bigger job opportunities awaited him elsewhere.

"How's your dad feeling since he got home from the hospital?"

"He's doing well, but he's as ornery as usual. I'm having more trouble keeping him in bed than he is having with his recovery." He snapped the carrot into three pieces and gave one to each animal. "Giving these horses to the city is very generous."

She patted Jake's back. "Our police department needs a mounted division like we used to have back when my Jerry was on the force."

"I'm all for it," he said. "You know I like riding." As if in invitation, the white horse snorted and nosed his shoulder.

"Tourist and residents loved seeing an officer patrolling the town square on horseback instead of a car. It added to the charm of our little town, and it gave people more of a chance to have a conversation with the officers and build a relationship." Mrs. Smith stroked the brown horse's neck, and he nuzzled against her touch. "Jerry thought it was important to let everyone know he was there for all of them."

"He was a wise cop and a great man. I learned a lot from Jerry." The words about building a relationship swirled in his head. He truly did want to have a good connection with all the citizens. And that included accident-prone women he met on the side of the road.

Mrs. Smith's smile was wistful, and she wiped a lone tear from her cheek. "I'll miss these beauties, but I'm looking forward to being close to my grandchildren."

He put an arm around her frail shoulders for a quick side hug. "That's understandable. We'll take good care of your horses. They will be boarded with Doc Ty Jackson until the old stables in town are repaired."

"How did it go when you talked to the city council about adding a K9 unit to the department?" she asked.

"Not great. They said it's not a good time, but if I buy a dog, I can be the first to have a canine partner. Specially trained dogs are very expensive, so it's a good thing I can do the training myself." But right now, he couldn't even afford a well-bred puppy.

"I expect so. But if anyone can figure out a way to make it happen, it's you."

He chuckled. "I appreciate the vote of confidence."

"That's what you did with the force in Dallas? Dog training?"

"Yes, ma'am. I became a master trainer right before Pops had his heart attack." Jake glanced at his watch. "I should probably get going so I can check on him."

"I've already got their harnesses on. Let me help you get them into the trailer."

Once Mrs. Smith said her goodbyes and the horses were loaded, Jake drove a few more miles back toward town. The local veterinarian, Dr. Tyrell Jackson, had his practice set up on his own ranch. Past his two-story stone house was his vet office with a large barn and stables tucked behind.

Doc Ty was already standing beside the trailer as Jake got out of the truck. "Howdy, Jake." The old cowboy shifted his hat.

"Hey, Doc. What's up?"

"A whole bunch of the usual and new stuff I hadn't planned on." He opened the trailer's sliding gate and stepped inside while Jake untied the horses' lead ropes from the outside. The veterinarian spoke to the animals in his usual kind way.

"All three look to be in good shape," Jake said.

"They are. I just gave them a checkup a few weeks ago. Mrs. Smith took real good care of all her animals."

"With help from several volunteers, we should have the town's old stables ready for them in a month or so."

Doc Ty let Jake take the first animal while he led out the other two. "The horses are welcome to board with me until construction starts."

The inside of the spacious barn was dark, and Jake

blinked to adjust his eyes. "What did you say your daughters are turning your ranch into?"

"A destination wedding venue with overnight cabins and all sorts of other stuff. The area behind the barn is being turned into a covered dance floor and bandstand. But I might have to talk them out of turning my surgical bay into a catering kitchen."

"That might be a good thing to keep around for emergencies. Sounds like a lot of changes."

"You're telling me." He put the black horse into an empty stall. "Also sounds like my retirement might be more work than I thought. Hopefully the new veterinarian will be able to help you out with the horses if the city doesn't have the stables ready in time. I know there's a nice horse barn on the place Dr. Talbot bought."

"Once he moves in, I'll go out and talk to him about it," Jake said.

The older man grinned and scratched his curly gray beard. "The new vet is a woman and she's arriving any day now. And she's very pretty."

Jake's belly whooshed as if he was on a roller coaster, but he wasn't sure why. "Then I'll go talk to her." He closed the last stall gate, and they walked out into the early-evening sunshine.

Did I just meet the new veterinarian on the roadside looking like a weary hitchhiker?

Chapter Two

"Somebody pinch me. I can't believe this place is really mine."

Jessica drove under a metal and timber archway at her new front gate, a stylized letter *W* decorating the center medallion. Although it originally welcomed one to the Williams Ranch, now the *W* would be in honor of her father, William Talbot.

The crepe myrtles lining the driveway had grown into impressive trees and were dressed in their spring best. Lavender and white blossoms lifted in a gust of wind and swirled around her like a welcome-home parade. With the release of a long-held breath, she could feel a mental weight lifting. Her life could move forward in whatever direction *she* chose. All the decisions were in her hands, and she'd be her own boss in every way.

Her tires rumbled across a metal-pipe cattle guard halfway down her driveway. The previous owner had grazed cattle in this area and having it fenced would come in handy for her wildlife rescue. Around a curve, her new house came into view. The spacious log cabin was set at the edge of the woods, framed by a backdrop of the hills.

She parked in the circle driveway in front of the cabin, and the first thing she did was get her cat out of the car. When she opened Oliver's carrier, he cautiously crept out, sniffed the air and then chased a lizard under a lantana bush covered with pink and yellow blossoms.

"You explore while I get us unloaded." She grabbed the first box and carried it onto the covered wraparound porch. This was the first home she'd ever owned, and the moment was bittersweet. The day her father had been killed protecting one of his movie star clients, she'd been on her way to tell him she'd put in an offer on the property they loved. But her chance to share her joy had been stolen.

The thought of her father made her turn toward the river. A gentle slope led down to the guest cottage where they'd spent three summers. Too bad it had been ruined by a flood. Her chest tightened, but instead of giving in to sad thoughts, she'd use the emotion to push forward. Her father would want her to be happy and celebrating. Unlike some people.

More than one person back in California told her

she shouldn't start such a large venture without a partner or spouse, but that only made her more determined to buy the place and prove she was capable of starting a business without the help of a husband. Growing up with her workaholic widowed father, and her Aunt Kay whose example was to allow her husband to control her, Jessica's idea of marriage was associated with heartache and a lack of independence. She'd been self-sufficient from an early age and needing someone was something she rarely let herself do. She'd be the first to admit that this cross-country move wouldn't be possible without her trust fund, but the rest she could handle. It was time to live the life of her choosing, on her own terms.

She unloaded her suitcases, sleeping bag with foam mattress and three boxes of important items like her coffeemaker, cat supplies, her mother's jewelry and the urn containing her father's ashes. Once everything was stacked on the porch, she pulled the key from her purse.

Oliver had done his business and now twined himself between her legs.

"Let's check out our new home and get you fed."

The lock clicked and the heavy wooden door swung open. Oliver led the way into the open-concept living space with its large fireplace. A sturdy timber mantel sat across the stone chimney that stretched up to the top of the vaulted ceiling where huge timber beams spanned the space. Beyond the living room, a dining area led to the gorgeous chef's kitchen. She hadn't been here in person for fourteen years, but the photos hadn't lied. The remodel was very well done.

A welcome basket from her Realtor sat on the kitchen island. It was filled with snacks, a candle and a bottle of wine. She brushed her hand across the sleek marble countertops and gazed out the wall of windows flanking the front door. All that glass would be a challenge to clean, but worth it for the view provided. Jessica walked through the two extra bedrooms and bath, then ended up in the master where the deep claw-foot tub was definitely calling her name.

Once the first box was unpacked, she fed Oliver, ate a snack and opened the bottle of wine. With a glass of pinot noir in hand, she filled the tub and added her favorite honeysuckle bubble bath. She groaned once again at her disastrous appearance but laughed when she found bits of bluebonnets stuck in her hair.

"What in the world must Jake think of me? My roadside performance was a movie-worthy comedic disaster scene."

Her lack of grace was nothing new, and although the embarrassment stung right now, it wasn't worth crying over. After raising the shade on the window beside the tub, she slipped into the sudsy water, the soothing warmth making her shiver with pleasure. There was no one close, so she could admire the view of the woods behind her cabin without fear of being seen. At least her day was ending on a high note. Inhaling the scent of honeysuckle, she began to wash away the grime of her crash refresher course in car maintenance.

Oliver pranced into the bathroom and stretched his long body to prop his paws on the rim of the tub. His meow ended on a purr, and he cocked his head while studying the bubbles.

"We can relax tonight, but we have a lot of work ahead of us. What do you say to putting bird feeders in those trees?" She scooped a handful of bubbles and held them toward her cat. After swatting them twice, he chased the floating bits around the room. "I need to buy a new tire, go to the grocery store, hire a contractor to build my office and exam room beside the barn and make a list of the million other things that need doing."

And I need to stop worrying about what Jake Carter thinks of me.

Jake returned the department's truck and trailer to the garage behind the police station and clocked out from his shift. Because he was running late after chatting with Mrs. Smith, then Doc Ty, he opted for takeout from the Acorn Café rather than cooking.

As he unlocked the front door of the house he shared with his dad, Seth Carter, the television greeted him with canned laughter from an old episode of *Seinfeld*. "How did you do today, Pops?"

"Good." His dad put a hand to the incision site on his chest, then turned down the volume. "I'll be as good as new by tomorrow."

Jake knew that wasn't true, but his dad had always been tough and stubborn as an old goat. This was possibly part of the reason his marriage didn't work, since Jake's mother was equally headstrong. "You had a heart attack and coronary bypass. This is the first time you've ever had surgery, and you're not used to taking anything slow and easy. But for once, you need to listen, or you'll end up back in the hospital."

"What did you bring? It smells good," Pops said to change the topic of conversation.

Jake knew he hated being fussed over and sitting still, but there was no other option. "Meat loaf, mashed potatoes and greens."

"What's on your sleeve? Looks like a handprint."

"It *is* a handprint. And it's probably going to leave a stain on my new shirt." Just as their brief meeting had made an impression that wasn't likely to fade any time soon. Jake glanced at his sleeve, and an image of the mystery woman flashed in his mind. Disheveled and sweaty, but…if his eyes hadn't fooled him, there was natural beauty under the smudges of dirt. As he'd held himself above her, with a blanket of bluebonnets beneath, he'd been close enough to see the golden starbursts in her catlike brown eyes.

"Did you get in a fight or get tackled by a wild animal?" Pops asked, pulling Jake from his thoughts.

Jake chuckled and set a container of food on the TV tray beside his dad's leather wingback chair. He'd been tackled, all right, but not by an animal. Although she had been a little wild. "Not exactly. I stopped to help a woman who was changing a tire on the side of farm road 1852."

"Did she wrap you in a big thank-you hug?"

"Something like that." There was no need to tell anyone that she'd taken him to the ground. But… he had prevented her from falling on her face. Jake grabbed his own meal and sat on the couch.

"Who was it on the roadside?"

"She's new in town. You haven't met her."

Pops grinned and pointed his fork at Jake. "I can tell by the look on your face that you're interested in her. I bet she's a looker."

"You'd be wrong." Guilt hit Jake square in the chest. He was trying to break his bad habit of judging people too quickly. The only fair thing was to give her another chance. Everyone had a bad day now and then, so he'd wipe the slate clean between them and the next time he saw her they could start fresh.

Why did he have a gut feeling Mystery Woman wasn't going to make that as easy as it sounded? Possibly because, for some unexplained reason, he couldn't stop thinking about her.

"You really should get back out there and date," his dad said between bites of mashed potatoes.

"Not you, too." His jaw muscles clenched. "Are you the one who put me on the radar of the town matchmakers?"

"Wasn't me."

His dad's grin cast doubt on that answer. "And you're one to talk. When is the last time you went out with a woman?"

Pops dismissed that with a wave of his hand. "I've already been married and had a kid."

Jake's stomach clenched. "I've been married, too. And you'll remember how that turned out?"

The burn of public humiliation still flashed whenever he thought about his ex-wife leaving without warning, then painting him as the bad guy. Just like she'd done with her family to get Jake to rescue her from what she'd claimed was a "terrible situation." Then when his very first arrest resulted in sending a town bully to prison, the guy promised retaliation against Jake's loved ones. She'd left a note by the coffeepot saying he put her in too much danger, and she wanted a divorce.

But he knew the truth. It had just been a convenient excuse to leave. Leaving was her go-to MO whenever she got bored.

With a deep inhale, Pops shook his head. "I know. I shouldn't have said that. But y'all were just kids right out of high school."

"I've had girlfriends since then," Jake said, then cut his meat loaf with enough force to puncture the bottom of the foam carton.

"Not in the last six months. I'll make you a deal. As soon as I'm one hundred percent healed, which should be real soon, I'll get back out there if you do. First one to go out on a date gets to pick the color we paint the house."

Jake perked up at that suggestion. They'd disagreed over the paint color for several weeks. "For real?"

"I've had a new lady at work smile at me a lot lately, and she's the one who brought the casserole yesterday. So, you better get a move on, son."

"Our small town doesn't exactly have a large dating pool." A vision of Mystery Woman popped into his head, and he squeezed his eyes closed as if that could hide the memory. A new woman had just jumped into the pool.

With the heavenly aroma of freshly brewed coffee hanging in the air, Jessica took her first sip. "Mmm. So good. One of my favorite things about mornings."

She stepped over her cat, and he followed her out onto the side deck that overlooked the huge, old oak tree and the gentle slope down to the river. The sun peeked over the hills, casting a colorful glow, and the air held a coolness that would soon be burned off by the April sunshine.

"Oliver, we need patio furniture. And maybe a couple of rocking chairs." Her cat walked a figure eight around her feet. "This is a view we'll never get tired of."

It was so nice to be out of her small apartment and away from the toxic work environment at her previous job. The owner of the fancy clinic and spa had turned up his nose at stray animals and hadn't let Jessica treat any of them in the building. He'd worried their wealthy clientele would leave for fear of a risk to their pets.

"Are you happy to be out in the country, sweet kitty cat?"

Oliver purred and rolled onto his back in a ray of sunshine, flipping his tail against her foot.

"I'll take that as a yes," she said with a laugh.

She hadn't been able to pass up the opportunity to own this ranch, especially since the property would feel like having her father with her again. Once she got settled, she'd find the perfect place to spread his ashes. Maybe at his favorite fishing spot where the large flat rock extended out into the river?

She drifted into memories of their fun summers in Oak Hollow. Those had been the few months of the year when he wasn't so busy with his company. He'd still talked to his team of bodyguards daily but had left time for the things he enjoyed. Time for cooking breakfast and riding horses with his daughter and fishing and hunting with his military buddy.

Oliver hopped up onto the railing and headbutted her arm in a not-so-subtle demand to pet him. The morning's peacefulness was interrupted when her cell phone played the song she'd programmed for her aunt's calls. Pulling it from the pocket of her robe, she answered.

"Hello, Aunt Kay."

"Good morning," she said in a big cheery voice. "How are you settling in?"

The joy her aunt projected made her smile. It hadn't been that way when her second husband was still around. "Everything is great." *If you don't count my unfortunate run-in with Officer Jake Carter.* "I'm going to spend the morning hiking around to see what's changed since I was here. Then in the afternoon, I'm expecting the moving truck. And this evening, my friend Emma is coming over."

"That sounds like a full day of fun. I wish I could be there with you."

"Don't worry about it for a second. You had to be there for your friend's wedding. Was it beautiful?"

"It was so elegant. I can't wait to help you plan your wedding someday."

"Might be a while." A long while. Jessica rolled her eyes and scratched her cat behind the ears. "Dating isn't a top priority for me, right now."

"I wish you'd reconsider. Surely there are some eligible men in your new town?"

"I'm sure there are, but you know me. I've always been okay with my own company."

"Jess, just promise me you'll stay open to possibilities."

She crushed a dried leaf under her foot. "Sure."

There was a moment of silence before her aunt cleared her throat. "I really hate to ruin your good mood, but I'm afraid I have a bit of…bad news."

Her aunt's heavy sigh struck a place of fear inside of Jessica. "Are you okay? Are you sick?" She couldn't bear to lose her quirky aunt so soon after her father. She was the closest thing to a mother that Jessica had ever had.

"I'm perfectly healthy. No need to worry about that. It's your trust fund that's the issue. I saw your request for a larger amount than usual, but your father put in…an unusual condition."

Jessica's stomach tightened, and a chill crept into her blood. "You're freaking me out. Just say it."

"If you want to withdraw more than the usual monthly amount all at once, you need to be married."

"Married?" Jessica's voice reached a shrill pitch that made Oliver leap from the railing and scurry away. The chill in her blood turned into a full-on ice storm. Unlike many fathers, hers had encouraged her to date and find a life partner, but this... "Why did he do this?"

"He loved you so very much, and he didn't want you to be alone like he was for so many years after your mother died. And of course, he didn't realize he would... That this would happen right when you bought a large piece of property and are starting your own practice."

Jessica was still speechless and staring out at the landscape. She'd been counting on withdrawing a larger than normal lump sum. Now what?

The jingle of Aunt Kay's metal bracelets cut through the silence on the phone line. "You still have enough savings to get started and hold you until your veterinary practice is turning a profit, right?"

"Yes." It was a bold-faced lie, but admitting the truth was too embarrassing. She'd used the last of her savings for the large down payment on this overbudget property. This trust fund issue was an unexpected hurdle, and at the moment, she had no idea how to clear it, but she had promised herself she would do this on her own.

"You're sure you'll be all right? You have enough money?"

"I'll be fine, Aunt Kay."

I will not be fine. This is a disaster!

She had fully intended to listen to her aunt's advice and not buy a piece of property overbudget, but a bidding war started, and she hadn't been willing to let this dream property slip through her fingers.

"Good. I'm glad to hear that you'll be okay. You've always been such a smart girl."

Apparently, not as smart as her aunt thought. A knot formed in Jessica's belly. "I need to go, Aunt Kay. I promise I'll call you soon."

She dropped her cell phone into the pocket of her robe, braced her elbows on the railing and covered her face. She not only couldn't wait for her veterinary practice to turn a profit, she didn't even have enough to *start* her practice. Maybe not even enough to make her monthly payments beyond a few months.

When she went back into the house to shove another donut—or four—into her mouth, the sunlight flashed off the silver metal of the urn holding her father's ashes. Her heart squeezed like it always did when she thought about not getting to him before he died, but this time it was tinged with a touch of anger, and she didn't like the feeling. He'd always been protective and more in her business than she'd liked, but she was a thirty-year-old woman who was very capable of deciding when or if she wanted to be married.

Grabbing the donut dusted with powdered sugar

and cinnamon, she sat on the countertop. Marriage had caused her father years of lonely heartache. Marriage had sapped the joy from her aunt. Another plus to their summers spent in Oak Hollow had been time away from watching Aunt Kay's controlling husband monitor every penny she spent and every place she went. Jessica would not let that happen to herself.

She put aside the donut and pressed her hands against her churning stomach. "I'm being a brat. I'm luckier than most to have any trust fund at all. I can figure this thing out." Her only option was to get a job and start saving up. And there was no time like the present. Exploring her property and finding a final resting place for her father would have to wait.

She took time doing her hair, leaving it loose with spiral curls swinging across her back. With makeup applied, she put on a knee-length blue dress and white sandals. She couldn't risk giving anyone else a disastrous first impression like her roadside performance for Jake.

After dropping off her car at the tire shop, she walked the few blocks to the center of town. The Oak Hollow town square had hardly changed since she'd been here. Shops ranging from quaint to quirky surrounded the center square, which held a gazebo and playground. And to her delight, much of the town's historic character had been kept intact. It might look picture perfect at first glance, but from her time here, Jessica knew this small town was more than the surface suggested. The citizens included all walks of life and a variety of unusual characters.

Spotting a help-wanted sign in the window of the Acorn Café, Jessica made her way closer. She'd never worked in a restaurant, and the sign didn't specify the job, but it couldn't be that hard. When she pushed through the door, a bell jingled above her head. A row of leather-covered stationary swivel stools lined the counter beside a bakery case. Taking a seat on one in the middle, she flipped open a menu to scan the options. There were all the usual Southern dishes like chicken fried steak and pot pies plus a variety of unique burger options.

The owner came out of the kitchen with a tray of cinnamon rolls that smelled divine. He had a touch of gray mixed in with his blond hair, but he was still handsome and still singing along with a country song. Judging from what she remembered, this should be a happy place to work.

"Welcome," he said with a wide smile and slid the tray into the bakery case. "What can I get for you today?"

"I would love one of those cinnamon rolls, a cup of coffee and a job."

He smiled and braced one hand on the countertop. "Guess you saw the sign in the window?"

"I did. What position are you hiring for?"

"A waitress. I'm Sam Hargrove. My wife and I own the place."

"I remember. I'm Jessica Talbot. I used to vacation here with my father years ago, and I've just moved to town."

"Welcome back to Oak Hollow. We are always happy to have new citizens. Do you have any experience working in a restaurant?"

"I don't, but I learn fast."

"If you have time now, after your coffee and cinnamon roll, how about an on-the-spot trial run? Since it's our slowest time between breakfast and lunch."

"I can do that. Thank you for the opportunity." After the morning phone call with her aunt, she was not going to let herself feel guilty about eating a cinnamon roll, even after the donuts.

Fueled by sugar and caffeine, she followed Sam into the kitchen, listened while he explained the basics and put on an apron. When they came out into the dining room, a young waiter said he'd just seated a table of three and they all needed coffee. Jessica poured three cups, rearranged them on the tray several times to get the balance just right and headed for the back of the restaurant. Two men faced her, but a partial booth divider blocked her view of the third person.

When she got closer and the third man came into view, her breath caught. She jolted just enough to tip the tray, and all three cups of hot coffee spilled directly onto Jake Carter's lap.

With a startled hiss, he jumped from his seat, banging his knee on the table hard enough to rattle everything.

"Oh my God." Jessica gasped and dropped the

tray onto the table, splashing more coffee in the process. She grabbed a handful of napkins before kneeling to pat him dry. When muffled chuckling came from behind her, she recognized what this must look like. Immediately backing away, she looked at the other two men, who she now realized were wearing police uniforms. They were attempting to suppress their laughter, but they were failing. Miserably.

Could this get any worse?

I should not *even be thinking that question.*

What was with her and her inability to be around him without doing something completely embarrassing or inappropriate? "I'm so sorry, Jake."

Before any of them had time to respond, she rushed away with flaming cheeks, apologized to Sam and left without glancing toward the booth of officers. On her walk back to the tire shop, she couldn't help laughing about the disaster scene she'd caused. If someone followed her around with a video camera, she could likely win money from the funny video program. As a kid, she'd learned it was better to let stuff like this roll off your back. Some things were just funny. Life was happier when you laughed along with others, even when it was at your expense.

But did it really have to involve Jake Carter? Again?

This could've been her opportunity to tell Jake who she was, and for him to see her looking so much better than yesterday. Her chance to make a new first impression had crashed along with cups of coffee.

Waitressing was most definitely off the table.

Chapter Three

Jake stood in the back of the Acorn Café with a throbbing knee, coffee-soaked and annoyed, while Anson and Luke made little effort to hide their laughter. The waitress had run away and might've been in tears. Since he'd mostly seen the top of her head as she tried to dry him off in an intimate way, he couldn't be one hundred percent sure, but Jake thought she was the same woman from the roadside the day before. The same one who had yanked him off-balance in an unexpected takedown maneuver.

Their usual waiter—who was also chuckling— tossed a towel to Jake and a second one to Officer Luke Walker. "I'll get some more coffee and bring it myself." He picked up the tray of dumped-over cups and walked away.

"Who's the new waitress?" Chief Anson Curry asked.

Jake shrugged and continued to blot coffee from his shirt and pants. "I have no idea."

But if she's my mystery woman, then she is well on her way to staining every uniform I own. Second chances or not, he'd be wise to steer clear of her and her accidents.

"But the waitress called you by name," Luke said and wiped the tabletop.

"She did?" Jake glanced around the café, but she was nowhere to be seen. "I'll go find out." He headed toward the front counter. When he still didn't see her anywhere, he opened the swinging door to the kitchen.

"Morning, Sam, where's the new waitress?"

Sam grinned. "You were the first and only table she served. She's gone."

Jake's eyes widened, and he stepped all the way into the kitchen. "You fired her just for spilling coffee?"

"Of course not. She quit." Sam flipped a burger and added a slice of cheese. "She just moved to town yesterday, and apparently waitressing is not for her."

Jake's skin prickled. What were the chances of two women moving to Oak Hollow on the same day? And judging by this second run-in, she had to be his mystery woman. "What's her name?"

"Jessica… I can't remember her last name. Good thing I'm not a detective."

"Thanks, Sam." Jake pushed through the swinging kitchen door, then paused behind the bakery case. Why did the woman who was determined to cause him bodily harm seem so familiar?

Before he could even slide back onto his side of the booth, he was hit with questions.

"Who is she?" Anson asked. "Did she finish drying you off…in private?"

"Ha-ha. No, Chief Smart-ass. Her name is Jessica, and she's already quit and left the building."

Anson and Luke quickly sobered, then looked at one another with a grimace.

"I hope it wasn't because we laughed," Luke said. "My wife gets annoyed when I laugh at her, but Alexandra is frequently doing something that makes me and Cody laugh."

"It certainly didn't help," Jake said.

Anson narrowed his blue eyes and rubbed a hand over his short blond beard. "Once we find out who she is, I'll apologize. It's just…of all the people for this to happen to, it had to be Mr. Clean. That will have to change once you have kids. My little one is always getting something on me. Yesterday it was finger paint and mud pies." The police chief's phone rang, and he pulled it from his pocket. "I knew I wouldn't get to stay and eat with y'all, but it looks like I'll be drinking coffee at the station."

"I'll pour yours into a to-go cup," the waiter called to them.

"Later, Chief," Luke said, then turned to Jake. "If this Jessica knows your name, you must have met her before."

"Or she just read my name on my uniform."

"She's pretty. It might do you good to find out more about her."

Even thinking any more about the mysterious Jessica was a bad idea. If he had anything else to do with her, she'd likely land him in the hospital.

After a long day of too much paperwork, Jake was glad to be home. He needed a cold drink and a hot shower.

"Hey, son."

His dad's voice came from the kitchen and the scent of food drifted his way. "Hi, Pops. What are you doing up and cooking?"

"I'm fine. Stop hovering like you're my nanny."

Jake wasn't going to admit that his dad appeared perfectly healthy. Standing to his full six-foot-two and his brown hair with barely a hint of gray, he looked younger than his fifty-six years. But he still needed time to heal from heart surgery.

"I heard about today's coffee mishap." Pops smiled and put pasta into the boiling water.

"Who called and told you about that?"

"No one. I was in the yard when Harold walked by, and he'd just seen his brother, who had lunch at the café."

Gossip traveled at warp speed in this town, and if he could find a way, he'd give it a speeding ticket. "And what were you doing out in the yard?"

Pops made a face. "Sitting on the porch like the invalid that you think I am."

"I just don't want you back in the hospital." The stack of medical bills was already higher than he cared to think about. And combined with unexpectedly needing to have the whole house rewired and replumbed right before he'd had the heart attack, money was tight.

"Stop worrying. Supper is almost ready."

On the way to his bedroom to change out of his coffee-scented uniform, Jake walked past the photos hanging in the hallway of his childhood home. He paused in front of one of him as a teenager with a group of kids at a town picnic. He squinted at the short girl with blue hair. Something clicked in his brain.

Jessica? Could Mystery Woman be the same girl I thought of as Summer Jess?

It had been years since he'd thought about the unusual girl who spent several summers in Oak Hollow, and he had no memory of her last name. To a small-town boy who'd been shy around girls, she'd seemed so...out of his league. She'd been petite with a different color and style of hair each summer. But mystery Jessica was only a few inches shorter than his six feet with long brown hair. And she hadn't said anything about knowing him.

Even though she'd been covered in dirt and sweat, when he'd looked down at her while braced above her in the bluebonnets, he'd had a surprising urge to kiss her. But why? She wasn't at all his type. His mother's voice played in his head. *Women should be perfectly groomed at all times.* Jake pinched the bridge of his nose. He was trying to stop thinking in the same way as his judgy mother. This wasn't the 1800s.

And from the glimpses he'd caught of Jessica the mystery waitress, her appearance was one hundred and eighty degrees opposite from the roadside version. If she even was the same woman. But he'd bet money that she was.

The moving truck had come and gone, and Jessica had been rearranging furniture and unpacking boxes for hours. Trying everything to burn off the memory of her extremely short career as a waitress.

"I should cut my hair into a pixie and dye it lime-green. Then maybe I could pretend I was a different new girl in town and start all over from the beginning."

Her cat hissed and batted the feathers on his indoor climbing tree.

"You're probably right, Oliver. Lime-green never did work with my complexion."

She carried a box of books to one of her two guest rooms. Even with some of the furniture from the Talbot family home, only one of the extra rooms had a bed, and it was twin-size. But there was no rush to get something better. No one would be staying with her any time soon. Above the sound of her music, a car door slammed, and she glanced at her watch.

"It's later than I thought. That must be Emma."

Their first summer vacation to Oak Hollow, she'd met Emma, and they'd become fast friends. She had introduced Jessica to more of the local kids, and it was at a party by the river where she'd first seen Jake. With his perfectly styled hair and trendy clothes, he had looked like he'd just stepped from the pages of one of the teen heartthrob magazines.

But Jessica… With silver braces and a body that was slow to develop, she'd been an awkward teen, especially around boys she was attracted to. She had dyed her hair fun colors to draw attention away from other areas such as her flat chest.

Hurrying to the front door, she went out onto the porch. Her childhood friend's long wavy blond hair was as pretty as ever.

Emma waved with her bright smile in place. "I'm so excited that you've moved to Oak Hollow. Sorry I was out of town and not here to greet you when you arrived."

"No worries. I've kept busy." *Busy making a complete fool of myself.*

Emma opened her passenger-side door and pulled out a pizza box and bottle of wine. "I brought the goat cheese, tomato and arugula pizza we talked about on the phone."

"Excellent. I'm starving and need a break from unpacking." Jessica took the bottle of wine and laughed. "Strawberry Fields. This is the wine we drank way too much of that last summer."

"That's because it was about a dollar a bottle."

"Oh, that's right." Jessica went up the two front steps. "Come inside. We have a lot of catching up to do. And what better way than with a glass of dollar wine. For old times' sake." They settled at the dining table and ate pizza right out of the box because she hadn't unpacked the plates yet.

"Some of the people you met years ago still live here, but there are also lots of new residents," Emma said and grabbed another slice. "I can't wait to introduce you to everyone in my book club. There are four of us, and sometimes we actually discuss the book along with laughing and drinking wine."

"That sounds perfect. I like reading, laughing and drinking wine."

"You'll fit right in. We meet at a bookstore called Sip & Read."

"I saw that place when I was in town but didn't have time to go inside. Tell me about some of the other new businesses since I was here."

With every place Emma told her about, Jessica took note of where she might seek out a job. She obviously wasn't qualified to work at a blacksmith shop—and had no idea such places were still around. And the butcher shop? She shivered at the thought. But the fabric store called Queen's Sew 'n' Sew and several other businesses on the square were on a possibility list.

Emma leaned back and pressed a hand to her stomach. "I have to stop eating." Oliver took her position as an invitation and hopped onto her lap. "Well, hello there. Aren't you a friendly kitty cat?"

"That's Oliver. He's a rescue and very sweet with people and other animals."

"He has such pretty orange markings. And speaking of hair, yours is so long and gorgeous," Emma said. "I don't think I've ever seen you with your natural color. Well, I'm assuming it's natural?"

"It is. Funny you should say that. I was just thinking I should change it as a disguise."

Her friend arched one blond eyebrow. "Why do you need a disguise? Who are you hiding from?"

Jessica took a sip of wine and started a retelling of her dramatically embarrassing last few days, and Emma was well entertained.

They moved out onto the deck to enjoy the beauty of a full moon casting silvery light over the countryside. Early spring crickets chirped, frogs sang from the direction of the river and rushing water completed the night melody. Oliver sat on the inside of the sliding glass door glaring at them, but she wasn't yet comfortable letting him out at night. A city cat needed more time to adjust to country life and its unique dangers.

"So, Jake is single?" *Why am I asking? I'm not here to find a boyfriend.*

"As far as I know. Unless he has someone back in Dallas that I don't know about."

"Dallas? He hasn't always lived here?"

"No. He only recently moved back. Maybe it's meant to be?"

"What's meant to be?" Jessica's brain started running through possible scenarios that she should not be entertaining.

"Your buying this ranch right after Jake moves home."

"I'm only curious about an old acquaintance, not

in the market for a man." Plus, police officer equaled danger, and danger equaled not being on her list of possible partners.

"And that's when love sneaks up on you. When you least expect it." Emma grinned and continued talking as if Jess had asked for his life story. "Just in case something does develop… Here's what I know. Jake joined the Oak Hollow police department right out of high school, then after a few years he got a job with a department in Dallas. That's where his mom lives. Jake moved back to Oak Hollow after his dad had a heart attack and then surgery."

"Oh, no. Is he okay?"

"Thankfully, yes. Seth Carter is a tough, hard-working guy, and I'm sure he'll be back to full activity, probably sooner than he should."

"So, he moved home to take care of his father and rejoined the Oak Hollow police department?"

"He sure did."

Jessica sat forward on one of the two cheap plastic lounge chairs she'd bought at the hardware store. "Jake really is one of the good guys, isn't he?"

Emma nodded and sipped her wine. "That he is. I haven't spent much time with him since he's come home. But I'm sure there's so much more for you to learn about him."

She decided to ignore the insinuation that she should hang out with Officer Carter. "Now that we've caught up on me and Jake, tell me how you really are. And not just the standard 'I'm fine' kind of answer."

Emma sighed and stared up at the stars, her smile fading into sadness.

Jessica's heart ached for her friend. She was still healing from the tragic loss of her husband and baby and would be for a long time. "If you don't want to talk about it, I completely understand. Forget I asked."

"Let's save that conversation for another day," Emma said. "I just want to focus on happy stuff tonight."

"We can do that." To lighten the mood, Jessica told more stories about times she'd done something clumsy in public.

The following morning, Jessica once again took extra care with her appearance before going into town. The number of parked cars was a good sign that business was booming in her new hometown. Fingers crossed that meant round two of her unexpected job hunt would bring success.

This quaint but thriving town square reminded her of tagging along to the movie studio as a child when her father checked on celebrity clients. Some of the movie sets had been like stepping into other worlds or times, and now she got to live it. The slower pace of Oak Hollow suited her much more than the glitz of Hollywood, and the more she interacted with her new home, it was clear that Oak Hollow was no boring, cookie-cutter town. It was modern and hip while retaining old-world whimsical elements.

She circled the square, and the only parking spot

was beside the courthouse…and right across from the redbrick police station. If you looked closely, you could see the faded words that revealed the building had once upon a time been a livery stable. Now she not only had Jake to blush in front of but also two more officers who'd witnessed her clumsiness. She probably already had a reputation around town. After locking her car, she walked around the hood of her SUV and was headed for Mackintosh's Five & Dime when something in the road caught her eye. A large turtle was making its way very slowly across the road toward the police station, and she could hear a car coming.

Jessica darted out into the road, scooped up the turtle and jumped out of the way in plenty of time, but not soon enough that she hadn't startled the driver. Breaks screeched, and she sucked in a sharp breath that caught in her throat. The car veered right, and the front corner of the bumper hit a metal trash can, causing an echoing clatter and a wave of garbage across the sidewalk—like an arrow pointing to the front door of the police station.

With an apologetic expression in place, she looked at the driver, and her stomach dropped to her toes. "Well, hell."

It wasn't just any driver or any old car. It was a police car. And one guess who was driving.

Chapter Four

Someone darted out from between two parked cars, and the sharp lash of alarm slapped Jake square in the chest. He jerked the steering wheel, swerved just a bit too far and hit one of the new trash cans the city had just installed. The clattering of metal hitting the sidewalk seemed to echo across the whole square, and the heat of embarrassment engulfed him. He was supposed to arrive at accident scenes, not be the one causing them.

"You have got to be kidding me." With his heart wedged tightly in his throat, he put the car in Park and spotted the person he'd almost hit. Not sure he should believe his eyes, he blinked a few times.

Mystery Woman?

She stood frozen in place, wide-eyed and holding… *Is that a turtle?* Was he being punked by the guys? With several groups of people hovering nearby to witness his humiliation, he got out of the car and inspected the front bumper, which thankfully had no damage.

When several smiling faces appeared in the front plate-glass window of the police station, he gave them a sufficient glare before turning to Mystery Woman. She had moved closer and was still holding her turtle—who was wisely tucked into his shell. Her face was almost as red as her ruffly blouse, and even in the currently unfortunate situation, he had to admit that she looked nice today. Beautiful actually. But from his personal experience, beautiful disaster was probably a more accurate description. And he avoided personal and relationship disasters at all costs.

Jake cleared his throat and broke the tense silence hanging in the air. "Which one of us are you trying to put in the hospital?" He was only half joking.

She bit her lower lip and shuffled one foot. "You have no idea how sorry I am or how much I wish I was invisible right now. But I had to save this turtle. At least there's one positive to this episode of 'How will she embarrass herself today?'"

A smile tugged at his lips. "There is?"

"I didn't mess up your clothes this time."

"True." He looked from his clean uniform to the trash on the sidewalk. "But I haven't picked that up yet."

"I'll do it…if you'll hold the turtle?" She glanced down at the animal in question.

He couldn't help but laugh. "I've never heard that one before. Is that like, hold my beer while I try this?"

"I guess so."

Her soft laugh made her eyes light up, and he had to look away before he forgot what he was doing. From the front seat of the car, he grabbed the empty cardboard box he'd used while delivering for Meals on Wheels. "Put him in this for now."

"Thanks." She gently placed the turtle inside the box. "You'll only have to stay in here until I find a safe place for you, big guy."

"He probably came from the coy pond beside the gazebo."

"I bet you're right." After cleaning her hands with the wet wipe he offered, she met Jake's eyes with a shy smile. "Of course, as I've unfortunately said several times over the last few days, I'll pay for any damages."

"No need. There doesn't seem to be any damage to the bumper or trash can." And thankfully none to her, either.

"Are you sure? I could volunteer at the police station to make up for this. And everything else I've done to you."

Whoa. That's a dangerous idea!

"No," he said a bit too eagerly, then saw her crestfallen expression. "I mean… That won't be necessary. But I will accept your offer to help me clean up."

"I'll do it all. You don't need to help." She looked

at the mess with her hands on her hips, then tipped her head from side to side as if forming a plan.

The combination of her movements and the way she'd been with the turtle sparked a stronger memory. The summer a visiting teenage girl punched a town bully—much larger than herself—when he threw a rock and knocked a bird out of a tree. She'd cried when she couldn't save it. And if he remembered correctly, she'd also saved a baby squirrel.

She is *Summer Jess.* "Jessica?"

"Yes?" She turned to face him.

He focused on her heart-shaped face and golden-brown eyes, and his pulse sped. "It *is* you. Jessica from California who came for the summers."

Her eyes widened, then a slow smile appeared. "Surprise. It's me."

"Why didn't you say anything?"

While smoothing the front of her shirt, she shrugged. "I could tell you didn't remember me, and I thought that was for the best, considering what happens every time I see you."

The station door swung open, and Luke stepped out onto the sidewalk, then handed Jake a broom and large dustpan. "Thought you might need these." He shifted his attention to Jessica. "Hi, I'm Luke Walker."

"Happy to meet you. I'm Jessica Talbot."

"I'd like to say sorry."

"For what?" she asked.

"For laughing yesterday in the café. We were laughing at Jake, not you."

"Oh, that." She glanced between them. "I guess it was one of those situations where it's hard not to laugh. But I should be the one apologizing. I probably got coffee on you, too."

"Nope. It all went on Mr. Clean."

Jake shot Luke a hard stare and started planning payback. "I think we've got it from here. Don't you have something you need to do?"

Luke grinned as he turned for the door. "See you around town, Jessica."

"Why did he call you Mr. Clean?"

"It's just a nickname they use to tease me. I'll hold the dustpan if you'll sweep." He did not want to go into details about his quirk. "You're the new veterinarian, right?"

"I sure am."

He righted the trash can. "I was planning on coming out to talk to you, before I knew it was you."

"And now you're too afraid for your life to come?"

"No. I just mean…" His throat tightened, and after fumbling with what to say, he caught her teasing expression.

"I know what you mean." She swept trash into the dustpan. "What did you want to talk about?"

"The horses. Can I put them in your barn?" *Pull it together, dude.* But it was hard when her glossy pink lips kept drawing his eyes like bees to flowers.

"Sure. You can put anything you want in my barn."

"Anything?" he asked and clenched his jaw to prevent a smile.

"If it fits," she said with all seriousness.

Her unintentional innuendo was too much, and his brain went straight where it shouldn't. He full on laughed, and at the same time hoped she wouldn't find him inappropriate.

Jessica's mouth dropped slightly open, but a second later she joined his laughter.

Most of Jake's tension melted away. It was refreshing to meet someone who could laugh at themselves—unlike his last one-sided, high-maintenance relationship. And thankfully Jessica hadn't taken offense when he turned a simple comment into something sexual. But who could blame a guy when it had been...way too long. Maybe everyone was right, and it was time to date again. But this time he'd take things extra slow and spend a lot of time getting to know the woman. His new slogan was *Cautious and slow,* just like a turtle.

And surprise. Summer Jess was turning out to be someone he hoped might be on board with his new unhurried dating tactic.

No sooner had Jake said goodbye to Jess and gone into the station's back kitchen area to grab a coffee when he heard a familiar female voice telling someone they needed to dust the leaves on the plant by the front door.

What is my mother doing here?

Jewels Carter usually called before making the trip from Dallas. He headed to the front and met her halfway for a quick hug. "Hey, Mom."

"Hello, son."

"I didn't know you were coming to town."

"Last minute trip for a friend's birthday, and I wanted to check on your father." She needlessly smoothed her blond hair, which was twisted into a fancy knot low on the back of her head, and her always assessing eyes scanned Jake from head to toe. "Your hair is a little long. Should I schedule a cut for you?"

And there it was. She couldn't even go one minute without pointing out something about his appearance or what needed improving. "No, thanks. Are you staying with me and Pops?"

"Yes, I talked to your father about it late last night."

Jake marveled at his parents' relationship. As much aggravation as his mother had given his father, Seth Carter still let her come stay in his house. They still argued, but since their divorce, it was more in good fun. They were better apart, but it hadn't gone unnoticed that they'd been talking more than usual.

"Do you have time for lunch?" she asked. "I'm not meeting my friends for another couple of hours."

Before Jake could decide how to answer, Anson walked up. "Hello, Mrs. Carter. How have you been?"

"Just dandy." She patted Anson's arm. "I told the new officer at the front desk to make note that the trim around the front door needs a fresh coat of paint."

Anson made a slightly strangled throat-clearing sound. "Noted. Jake, go have lunch with your mom and please bring me a burger and fries. I have to be on a conference call for the next hour."

"Will do." Jake knew his friend was also asking him as politely as possible to get his busybody mom out of the station before one of them was tempted to give her a police escort all the way back to Dallas. "Where do you want to eat?"

"The Acorn Café. Up in my part of the state, I can't get peach cobbler like they make."

Jake held the door for her, and they stepped out into the midday heat.

As they crossed the center of the square, she glanced at his feet. "You need new boots. Those are scuffed and worn."

"They're not that old. And they're combat boots. I'm wearing them to work, not church."

"You should always look your best."

His mom believed you should always have shiny shoes, and he used to live by that, but he'd started to ease up on himself. Her unannounced pop-in inspection was not what he needed after the progress he'd made.

The bell above the door chimed on entry, and luckily they'd beat the lunch rush.

"We should sit in a booth by the window," she said.

This was code for keeping an eye on what was happening outside, lest she miss something that needed her opinion.

"So, tell me, who are you dating?" she asked while rearranging the condiments.

That didn't take long.

"No one at the moment." No way in hell was he

going to tell Jewels Carter he was considering taking his time getting to know Jessica.

"You're young and healthy and should have no trouble dating. When are you going to try again and give me some grandchildren? My younger sister already has three." Her red fingernails clicked against the turquoise Formica tabletop.

"I have no timeline on giving you grandchildren. But you'll be the second to know."

"Second?" Her forehead furrowed as much as it could after Botox injections.

He chuckled. "The mother of my children will be the first to know."

"Oh, of course. And no idea who that could possibly be?"

"Nope." Her line of questioning was added proof he shouldn't subject Jessica to his mother's scrutiny. Not if he expected his mystery woman to stick around for an extended get-to-know-you period. But that was probably a moot point because he wasn't sticking around Oak Hollow for long.

His mother would no doubt treat the situation with Jessica as if it were a job interview. Jake loved his mom, but he took a deep breath and prepared himself for a long lunch of chicken-fried steak with a side of well-intentioned criticism and an added dash of guilt.

Trying very hard not to think too much about Jake and his supersexy smile, Jessica abandoned her job search and drove out into the countryside. This most recent interaction had started out horribly, but before they'd said goodbye, they'd both been smiling and laughing.

Was Jake flirting with me?

Finding the turtle had given her an idea. If a little luck would shine her way, maybe Dr. Tyrell Jackson was looking for some help with closing out his practice? And if not, she could ask what he thought about starting a mobile vet business and traveling to her clients. She didn't want to step on his toes or steal patients without talking to him first.

She drove another mile and turned onto the paved driveway of Dr. Jackson's impressive ranch. When they'd met at a conference and he'd told her he was from Oak Hollow and retiring soon, she couldn't believe her luck. It had been another reason she'd blown her home-buying budget out of the water. But the opportunity to step in and fill the void his retirement would create had been another sign she could not ignore.

Jessica pulled to a stop in front of a tan metal building with Dr. Jackson's name and information on a big wooden sign.

He waved from the front door of his office. "Afternoon, Dr. Talbot."

"It's so nice to see you again, Dr. Jackson." They shook hands.

"Everyone around here just calls me Ty or Doc Ty."

"I like it. Casual and not too stuffy." *Like the last place I worked.*

"Come on inside and get out of the heat." He motioned for her to follow. "Let me grab a couple of cold

drinks." Behind the front desk, he opened a small refrigerator and pulled out two bottles of water, and then
the phone rang. "Let me grab this call real quick."

"No problem."

He was just as friendly and upbeat as she remembered from his presentation at the conference. Lucky
for her, she might have a chance to learn from his
skills and techniques before his retirement. Back in
Los Angeles, she'd treated pets that included expensive horses in pricy stables and a few exotics, but not
cows and chickens. There hadn't been much call for
that in Beverly Hills.

Who knows what kind of animals she could've
worked with if she'd taken the job at the MGM movie
lot? But if she had accepted that job, she would've
missed the opportunity to buy her dream ranch.
What she'd once thought was a huge mistake had
become a blessing that led her to Oak Hollow. Still,
she regretted passing up something she really wanted
because of a guy. Espccially a guy who turned out
to be a total jerk.

Don't think about that or him right now!

Ty handed her an ice-cold bottle of water. "How
are you settling into our little town?"

"Very well." There was already so much she could
tell him. It was enough to start her own slapstick comedy routine. "I'm still unpacking and meeting people."

"There are lots of good folks around these parts."
He walked through the reception area to a hallway.

"I can tell. I've been thinking about a way to meet
more of them. Are you still planning to retire?"

"I sure am." He moved from room to room giving her a tour without needing to explain what they were seeing. "Probably fully in about six to eight months."

"Are you by any chance looking for an assistant until then?"

His full gray eyebrows arched. "Thought you were starting your own practice?"

"Oh, I am, but..." She hesitated with what and how much to say. "I thought it might be a good way to meet people and give them a chance to trust me with their animals. And it will be a while before I have my clinic built." Every word of that was true. She'd only left out the money part.

He propped his hands on a stainless-steel exam table. "That makes sense, and it's a real good idea. There will soon be so much going on around my place that I could actually use the help. My daughters are turning part of the ranch into a destination wedding venue."

"It's certainly a lovely spot for that."

"Let's sit in my office and we can discuss the details."

She sat across from Doc Ty and had a great view of all his certificates and degrees on one wall and photographs along the top of the file cabinets. Someday she'd have her own office. Maybe not as soon as she'd hoped, but someday.

And thirty minutes later, she left with a part-time job.

Before heading home, Jessica stopped at the grocery store to stock up on all the essentials and baking ingredients to make her famous banana walnut bread. It would give her a reason to go to the police station and hopefully be a good way to apologize for all the trouble she'd caused Jake. Everyone liked her banana bread, so surely Jake would, too.

Jessica had been to the square enough that she had a pretty good feel for the pulse of the town on a weekday morning. Instead of rushing straight over to give Jake the banana bread, she slowed her steps and took everything in. The florist was loading flower arrangements into the back of a van, and the sweet aroma followed her as she passed. A couple of pre-teens wearing backpacks ran by, arguing about which one of them forgot to set the alarm clock. People dressed for work moved at a brisk pace, going in the Acorn Café and coming out with to-go cups and bags of what were probably those divine cinnamon rolls. But it was nothing like the endless stream of Starbucks customers she was used to.

She said hello to a group of moms pushing strollers and crossed the street. The police station sat on a corner of the square with ivy climbing one side, and as she pushed through the front door, her heart beat so fast it threatened to bruise her breastbone.

Why am I so nervous?

She hadn't even known for sure if Jake would be at work this morning, but there he was, sitting at a brown metal desk, his back to her while talking on the phone. Compared to the stations in movies and television, this small-town version was homey and at least for the moment not chaotic at all. In front of her sat a built-in reception desk, a wooden half wall running from the desk to the opposite side of the room. To get beyond, you entered through a waist-high swinging door.

A woman with a gray pixie cut and big smile was standing behind the front desk. "Good morning. Can I help you?"

"Good morning. If it's okay, I'm just waiting to talk to Officer Carter once he's off the phone?"

"Sure. You can have a seat over there." She pointed to a row of wooden chairs lined up along the wall with potted plants and watercolor paintings hanging above.

"Thank you." Jessica chose the chair closest to Jake and could now hear his side of the phone conversation. She had a moment of guilt for eavesdropping, but if it was private, he wouldn't be having it right out in the open.

"The dog cost how much?" He groaned and rubbed the back of his neck. "Did you say between $30,000 and $50,000? There goes that dream. I could never afford a police dog that expensive. The unexpected costs have been piling up around here. On top of the mountain of medical bills, a water leak turned into a full replumbing of my dad's whole house. And that's after he'd just had it rewired a month before." Jake twirled a pencil around his fingers while listening. "No, I can't come back to the K9 unit until my dad is one hundred percent back on his feet and I know he's taking care of himself." Jake's bark of laughter made several people look his way. "What do you expect me to do? Find a rich wife to solve my problems?"

Jessica sat up straighter, catching the loaf of banana bread before it tumbled from her lap.

Don't even think it, girl!

Nevertheless, an idea—a very, very bad idea—flicked on with the brightness of stage lights.

I'm here to start a business, not get myself into a...situation.

Now was not the time for a romance. Real or pretend.

Or was it exactly the right time?

Jake leaned back in the squeaky office chair. "I have to help my dad. His new heart medication is ridiculously expensive." At that moment, he turned and caught sight of Jessica and his eyes widened. "I need to go. I'll call you later." He motioned for her to come through to the back area.

Jessica walked toward him with her gift held out. "I brought you a peace offering. It's banana nut bread." Their fingers brushed as he took it and a tingle spread up her arm. The quick flare in his blue eyes made her think he'd felt it, too.

"Thank you." He brought it to his nose. "It smells great. What kind of nuts are in it?"

"Walnuts."

He cleared his throat and gave her a half grin. "I'm allergic to walnuts."

Of course he is.

Jessica was tempted to grab the bread and drop it

into the trash can. Instead, she took a deep breath. Why couldn't she get anything right with this man? "I swear I'm really not trying to land you in the hospital with an allergic reaction to walnuts."

"I'm not allergic to walnuts," said the blond-haired officer she'd seen at the café.

She took the bread from Jake and put it into the other man's hands. "Excellent. I hope you enjoy it."

"I'm sure I will. I'm Chief Anson Curry. I hear you'll be joining my wife and the others for their girls' night?"

"Yes, Emma invited me. She's the only one in the group that I know. Who is your wife?"

"Tess. She runs the antique store next door." He hitched his thumb to his right.

"Great. I'll stop in and see her. My new house is bigger than I thought, and I could use a few more pieces of furniture." *Too bad I can't afford it right now.*

"Chief," said the woman behind the front desk. "I need you to see this."

"Excuse me. It was nice to meet you."

"You, too." When Chief Anson Curry walked away, awkwardness swirled in the air between her and Jake. "Okay, then. I guess I'll see you around." She turned to leave and maybe never come back.

"Wait," Jake said. "Thanks for the thought. I'm sure it's delicious. Wish I could eat it."

"I'm just glad you asked about the nuts. I would have to move out of town if I actually put you in the hospital."

He shrugged. "The walnuts wouldn't put me in the hospital. They just make my mouth break out. I've been told to avoid them."

When someone called Jake's name, Jessica made her getaway, moving at a pace just under attention-drawing speed. First step onto the sidewalk, she was hit with a warm Texas breeze that tossed her hair around her shoulders. She started walking without any thought of where to go. Her mind was too busy barreling toward what was likely a disastrous destination.

Am I honestly thinking about asking a police officer to consider a marriage of convenience?

Chapter Five

Jake intended to walk Jessica to the front door of the police station and pick a time to visit her ranch and discuss boarding the horses, but she rushed away like she'd been standing on hot coals. By the time he made it to the sidewalk, she was already three stores down, her long hair swinging rhythmically across her back, and naturally drawing his eyes lower.

He tugged at his collar. Had someone just turned up the heat by ten degrees? Her dark jeans certainly weren't the shapeless ripped ones she'd worn on the roadside. This pair fit just right. Jake pressed his fingers to his eyes, forcing himself to stop watching her like a lusty teenager. He was correct about natural beauty hiding under the dirt and baggy clothing of their first meeting. She did not look like a woman in need of rescue today. If he wasn't careful, he'd be the one who needed rescuing.

The mystery of her identity was solved, but who had Summer Jess become?

Do I really want that answer?

With a deep sigh, he admitted that he did. He was cautiously curious, but who could blame him for the concern when every encounter left him dazed and confused. Considering recent intel, the potential for disaster was abnormally high. Jake went back inside and grinned at the sight of three people already eating banana bread. By the looks on their faces, it was good. He'd have to remember to tell her. But it might be wise to take someone with him when he went out to her ranch.

Anson jingled a set of keys in front of Jake's face. "No daydreaming on the job. Ride the morning route with me."

"Let's go." A distraction was exactly what he needed.

They went out the back door to the fenced parking area behind the station, and Jake climbed into the passenger seat.

"Did you ask her out?" Anson clicked his seat belt into place.

"Who?" Jake asked—knowing full well they were talking about Jessica.

"Who do you think? The pretty woman who's had your attention for the last few days."

"I might need to up my life insurance first. And she's drawing my attention because I'm trained to watch out for danger."

Anson laughed and pulled out of the parking area, then headed away from the square. "It couldn't be all that bad."

"You recall yesterday's trash can incident?" The back of his neck and ears grew warm at the memory, but when Jake envisioned her standing there wide-eyed with that turtle, he smiled.

"I did hear about your fender bender. From everyone."

"I bet they were all too eager to tell you and probably embellished the story by a mile." They rode in silence for the next few minutes, neighborhoods giving way to ranchland and grazing animals. Jake rolled down the window as they passed by Green Forest Nursery. Warm air rushed in, carrying the scent of freshly turned earth and a hint of rain in the air.

Anson rolled down his own window and made the turn to circle back toward town. "I couldn't help but notice the way Jessica was looking at you today. Especially while you were on the phone."

Pressure built in Jake's chest. "I'm not sure I like the sound of that. What kind of look?"

"Like she was taking notes and planning your wedding."

"Dude, do not even say that."

Anson chuckled. "I'm just messing with you. But I'd say it's a pretty safe bet she's coming around for more than an apology."

"I'm not jumping into anything with anyone. Lately, I've been a magnet for women who get attached immediately and want way more than is reasonable too early in the relationship."

"Your last few girlfriends have been extra clingy," Anson said and waved to an older couple out for a morning walk.

"Why do you think I refer to the most recent one as Miss Velcro?"

"Like the time she left wedding magazines on your desk at work?"

"Exactly." Jake glanced at his left hand and could barely remember what his wedding ring had looked like. Had it been silver or gold?

"I'm so glad I'm married and don't have to deal with that stuff anymore," Anson said.

"Marriage didn't keep that from happening in my case. Yours is working because Tess is a wonderful woman."

"Can't argue with that. But there are more amazing women out there." The other man's grin had gone from teasing to understanding. "Tess is what I was missing. And Hannah, too. Hearing her sweet little voice calling me Daddy is one of the best things ever."

"You wouldn't know by watching you together that Hannah hasn't been yours from birth. Do you plan to have more kids?"

"We've been trying. Just hasn't happened." Anson's sigh was heavy. "I'm going to pass along what I've learned. Remember, I was married before, and it wasn't good. But don't let bad experiences with women keep you from trying again. Maybe set some relationship expectations right up front."

"Have you been talking to my dad?" Jake asked.

"No. Why?"

"Pops was saying the same kind of stuff last night."

"You should listen to the older and wiser men in your life. Myself included."

Jake adjusted his seat belt. "I think the town matchmakers have declared me their newest target. It's making me want to move back to Dallas sooner than planned."

"I'm still hoping you'll change your mind and stay, but I understand your reasons for going back. I also remember the pressure from that group of well-meaning matchmakers," Anson said. "I'm sure my grandmother, Nan, is in on it, too."

"Good. Maybe you can tell her to take me off their list." Jake stared out the car's side window. Things he'd seen his whole life whipped by like a child's flipbook. A rapid trip down memory lane.

Each encounter with Mystery Woman left him a little more curious and intrigued. He joked about the danger she posed, but if they took things beyond friendship, the real danger could be to one of their hearts. He'd be returning to Dallas at some point, and starting a romantic relationship was a setup for disaster and heartache. His pulse quickened. But with the emotions Jessica awakened... He found himself weighing the risks.

Cautious and slow.

He needed to start repeating that as a morning mantra. Maybe morning, noon and night.

"The next woman I date, I'll make it clear that I plan to take any relationship nice and slow. And maybe keep things casual."

Jessica turned down the Celine Dion song on the radio and parked on the opposite side of the square from the police station. It had been less than eight hours since she fumbled the banana bread apology, and all she'd been able to think about was Jake's side of his phone conversation. If she turned his joke about needing a wife into a reality... It could be the answer to her trust fund problem. But at what cost?

Her respect? The thought of Jake was enough to make her whole body warm. If she wasn't careful, the price could be her heart. But they needed the same things. Enough money to pay bills and follow their dreams.

When Jessica walked through the double doors of Sip & Read, the aroma of coffee, flowers and that magical scent of books made her smile. According to the historic marker she'd read before entering, the two-story building had originally been a hardware store in the 1920s, then a dress shop, a restaurant and now this unique bookstore. An eclectic mix of shelves were artfully arranged into genre-specific areas with decor and merchandise tailored to each section.

Emma waved from a round table off to one side, and Jessica made her way across the store. Her childhood friend was seated in the romance section. It was decorated with flameless candles, flowers, a pink velvet couch and two tables with mismatched wooden chairs.

"This place is the coolest bookstore ever," she said and glanced up to the high ceiling, covered with pressed tin squares.

"It really is. The owner worked in the book publishing industry before moving back to Oak Hollow. Then he bought this building and renovated it. If you look closely, you'll see photos of famous authors all around the store." Emma pointed to the brick wall, partially covered with old plaster that had chipped away in large chunks. "There's one of Nora Roberts."

"I love it. I noticed a few others on my way over." She'd also noticed several novels with wedding and marriage in the title. A Wedding Made for Her. His Arranged Marriage. Even the books were encouraging her toward a conversation with Jake.

"I ordered a bottle of wine, but I waited to order food." She slid a small paper menu in front of Jessica. "One side is appetizers, and the other is desserts."

Jessica looked over the options. "The sampler platter sounds good, and later, we can end with coffee and one of these delicious-sounding desserts. I might have to try the pecan pie cheesecake."

"It's a-ma-zing. And the pecans grow locally."

Another woman waved from the doorway and breezed gracefully toward their table like a runway model. Her halter-neckline emerald dress flowed loosely around her body and the color looked fabulous with her gorgeous red hair.

"Hi, you must be Jessica. I'm Alexandra Walker," she said and hung a large, fringed purse on the back of her chair.

"So nice to meet you." It wasn't until Alexandra cradled her belly before sitting that Jessica realized she was pregnant.

"How are you feeling?" Emma asked her. "Are you having any new weird cravings?"

"Yes. Watermelon and potato chips. Together."

Jessica had been reluctant to say anything on the topic of babies, unsure how Emma would react after her loss. It was a relief to see that her friend could smile while talking to a pregnant woman about her symptoms.

"Here comes Tess," Emma said and pointed toward a woman with wavy brown hair and a wide smile that showed off deep dimples.

She gave off a Jennifer Garner vibe, and Jessica had a feeling they'd get along well. After the final introductions were made, they ordered fried zucchini, bruschetta and a cheese board.

"It will just be the four of us tonight," Emma said. "Jenny has last-minute wedding stuff to do."

Alexandra blew steam from her cup of herbal tea. "She is supposed to ask us for help with wedding stuff."

"This was something she had to do herself. It's her final dress fitting." Emma put another piece of bruschetta on her plate. "They're having the ceremony and reception at their house, and it the weather cooperates, it will be outside."

Tess's laugh matched her wide smile. "When she says house, she means the amazing Barton Estate with a gorgeous 175-year-old house that her fiancé is restoring to its original splendor. Being a history buff, I get more excited than the average person about this. It's going to be such a romantic wedding."

"That sounds amazing." Jessica's knee bounced under the table. Since Aunt Kay's call, references to marriage were everywhere. Was she only noticing because it was on her mind or was it a sign that she should do something about her marital status? If so, expanding her prospects beyond one person wasn't a bad idea. Jake wasn't the only guy in town. There were likely other men who did not have hazardous jobs.

"What can you tell me about the single guy situation in Oak Hollow?"

"There isn't a huge pool to choose from," Alexandra said while looking for something in her large purse. She pulled out sheets of music, a set of watercolor paints and nail polish before finding her lip balm. "I recently married one of the good ones." Her sigh was one of those satisfied and dreamy sounds only made by a woman in love.

"I got it right when I married Anson," Tess said. "Thank goodness I came to my senses before he gave up on me."

"There's no way Anson was going to give up on you." Emma topped off her wine. "He adores you."

While Jessica was happy for her new friends, an ache kicked up in her chest along with a touch of jealousy. Not because a husband would give her access to the money she needed to keep her ranch, but because, if these women were any indicator, having a partner in life might not be so bad, after all.

Jake's face popped into her mind for the thousandth time today and something fluttered in her stomach. Her sudden reevaluation of matrimony surprised her more than a little bit. Whatever the reason, it sure would make her father happy. Jessica glanced upward, wondering if he was looking down and somehow guiding things in a certain direction.

The local Fredericksburg peach wine tickled Jessica's tongue with tart sweetness, but when the man in the Home Improvement section turned around, she almost choked on the sip.

Emma, Tess and Alexandra stopped talking and followed her gaze.

Jake was flipping through a large book with tools on the cover. In well-worn jeans and a black T-shirt, he looked as if he should be on the cover of a romance novel. The kind where tattoos peek from his shirtsleeve. He was sexy in a bad boy kind of way and her fingers flexed with a desire to touch him.

So much for getting my mind off him tonight.

He closed the book and took a few steps, but Jake paused, and his eyes widened as he caught them staring. "Evening, ladies." His voice was as smooth as fine whiskey, but his expression told a different story.

The chorus of female "hellos" seemed to increase his speed toward the cashier.

There were a few beats of silence before Alexandra spoke. "He's good looking, right?"

"Who? Jake?" Without letting her eyes drift toward the cashier, Jessica shrugged as if it didn't matter and her heart wasn't racing. "I guess so. The first time I met him was over fourteen years ago. I used to spend summers here with my father."

"And what was it you told me about Jake when I came over with pizza the other night?"

With a wine induced giggle, Jessica rubbed her warm cheeks. "That I might have had a small crush on him."

Tess's diamond ring clinked against the stem of her wine glass. "Did you move to Oak Hollow alone?"

"I did. Just me and my cat, Oliver."

"You're single?" Tess and Alexandra asked in unison.

"I am." Sounds like I'm well on my way to becoming the spinster cat lady. Even if she talked Jake into her unorthodox fake marriage plan, they wouldn't have a wedding like the one these women described. Because it wouldn't be real.

"Jake is single, too," Alexandra said in a singsong voice. "Was he happy to see you again?"

The warmth of a blush spread across Jessica's face, and she laughed without real amusement. "It took him a while to remember me. At first that was a good thing because I do something embarrassing every single time I see him."

"I heard about that," Tess said.

A jolt zipped along her spine. With her recent blunders, she'd worried about getting a reputation as the accident-prone new girl. Laughing off a few mishaps was one thing but becoming the town laughing-stock was an entirely different beast. "Is the whole town laughing at me?"

"Oh, no, no. I'm sorry. That's not what I meant. I only know because Anson told me. Embarrassing things happen to all of us at some point. A few weeks ago, I tripped and fell flat on my face while walking across the playground," Tess said, and they all laughed.

Jessica released a breath. These women weren't judging her like some of the people in California. They'd welcomed her into their group of friends, and the laughing was done together, not at one another's expense.

"You're just collecting funny stories to tell when you're old," Emma said. "Speaking of stories, let's pick our next book."

Jessica glanced once more toward the front of the store, but Jake was long gone.

Does he even give me a second thought?

He certainly hadn't rushed over for her phone number.

After a restless night of strange dreams, Jessica had been dragging all day. They had been those annoying dreams that go on and on, loop back on themselves and never have a satisfying ending. Jake had been the star of the show, and of course she'd done one embarrassing thing after another. Everything from realizing she was in public without clothes to spilling things on Jake, and worst of all, walking down the aisle to discover there was no groom.

Her sleep disruption was no doubt due to a combination of wine and then caffeine from their round of coffee and dessert. Add that to her need of a spouse and the discussion about marriage and dating with her new friends at book club, and it was the perfect storm. And walking laps around her house wasn't helping her state of mind. She'd started six different text messages to Jake and erased all of them.

"Is a marriage of convenience an absurd idea?" she asked her cat, but Oliver had grown tired of keeping pace and settled down for a nap on the maroon couch.

Her options were limited. She could tell her aunt the truth of her mistake, but that would disappoint her and make all the doubters say they'd told her so. If she saved as much money as possible each month, she'd hopefully be able to keep the ranch and maybe have enough to start her business in a few years. The thought of waiting that long was disappointing, but probably a better idea than trying to find a husband in a hurry. She shuddered at the idea of joining a dating app.

"Too bad there isn't one called Get Hitched Quick." She laughed at the ridiculousness of that idea and walked another circle through her living area before stopping in front of the huge windows.

Late-afternoon sunlight cast long shadows across the front yard. The gorgeous view relaxed her tense muscles.

"I can't lose this ranch. It's not an option." She would not go back to California as a failure. So, the conclusion of today's thought fest was to find some courage and at least talk to Jake about the idea of a mutually beneficial arrangement.

"How does a person go about asking someone they hardly know to marry them?" It wasn't like she'd be asking an officer of the law to do something illegal, but it wasn't exactly ethical. However, if they could come to an agreement, it would benefit both of them. Jake could pay hospital bills and buy the expensive police dog.

Was it just wishful thinking that she felt chemistry between them? Maybe if they spent more time together...

"No. Back it up, girl." She could not let herself hope for romance or true love. Not after her latest relationship fail. She hadn't been Beverly Hills enough for her most recent ex, and he'd shown his true nature when he left her with offensive parting words. *"You're the kind of woman a man dates. You don't have the qualities to be a wife or have a long-term relationship."*

She ran her fingers roughly through her hair. "That's over, and I've moved on to better things and people."

But those cutting words had left a scar.

Whether she talked to Jake about her wacky plan

or not, she still needed to arrange a time for him to see her barn. It would be an opportunity to have a normal human interaction without causing a scene. A gauge for how to move forward. *If* things went well, she'd see about asking this mega favor.

"By the way," she said in a dramatic voice. "Now that we've talked about the horses, would you like to get married? For money?" Jessica laughed and then groaned before flopping onto the couch.

The cushions bounced and Oliver startled awake with a side-eyed glance and a wide yawn.

She stroked his soft fur until his purr motor turned on. "I'm overthinking this, aren't I? I'll just see how it goes and take it from there."

Grabbing her phone from the coffee table, she pushed her jumbled thoughts aside and typed out a message.

This is Jessica. Hope you don't mind that Emma gave me your number. When would you like to come and see my barn?

She hit Send, then gasped at the last sentence. "No, no, no." How had she written this after they'd so recently laughed at her unintentionally suggestive *"you can put anything in my barn...if it fits"* comment?

"For the love of donuts. I don't even have to be in the same room with the man and I still manage to embarrass myself."

Would he think she was hitting on him? Was she?

The dots that told her he was typing appeared on her screen. Then they disappeared. "He's probably laughing too hard to type." And then the dots were back, and a message arrived.

Can I come over right after work?

Thankfully, there weren't any laughing face emojis. Her heart rate sped. "I need to get a grip. It's not like he's saying yes to my marriage proposal." After a deep breath to calm her butterflies, she sent a short reply.

That works for me.

And then she went to touch up her makeup and change into something more flattering than her yoga pants and faded concert T-shirt.

Chapter Six

Jake drove out to Jessica's ranch—without his antici-
pated backup. At the last moment, Anson had mum-
bled some lame excuse that Jake wouldn't buy for a
penny. It was as if the town matchmakers had written a front-page headline in the *Oak Hollow Herald*
declaring Jake Carter Needs a Date, and apparently
they'd recruited his buddies.

He hadn't been nervous around a woman in years.
Mystery Woman might be dangerous, but she was
also entertaining and able to laugh at herself. Miss
Velcro had not been able to do that and had pouted
if anyone laughed at something she did or said. That
had become a drag in a hurry.

Jessica's house came into view, and even from a

distance he could tell that the large expensive-looking barn was more than adequate to house the horses.

This trip wasn't necessary.

He could've taken Doc Ty's word that the barn would work. But here he was, and he was not going to dive into why his brain chose to keep this fact a secret until now. He parked his truck beside her SUV and his stomach suddenly felt hollow.

"I'm just hungry."

When she stepped out onto the porch and his mouth went dry, he knew it was more than hunger for food. But his curiosity was too strong to abort the mission now. And it wasn't like she'd finally finish him off this time. The thought of her doing something funny made him smile.

When he got out and closed his door, they shared an awkward wave.

"Thanks for letting me come out and take a look. And for being willing to take on the horses so soon after moving in."

"No problem. I love having animals around."

As if to prove her point, an orange cat bounded from under a bush and shot up the side of an oak tree like a wildcat on the hunt.

Oh, man, I should've guessed she'd be a cat lover.

He'd never been much of a cat guy, especially after one climbed his leg, leaving a trail of bloody claw marks. He hadn't touched one since. And the way her pet climbed was proof he could make Jake's fear come true.

"That's Oliver. He's showing off his climbing

skills." She crossed and uncrossed her arms, then smiled shyly.

So, he wasn't the only one whose nerves weren't playing nice. The scent of vanilla and brown sugar drifted out the open front door. "Did you bake more banana bread? Everyone really liked it."

"I baked cookies this time. Chocolate chip with no nuts." She tucked her long hair behind her ear and seemed to be having trouble meeting his eyes. "Would you like some?"

His stomach chose that moment to growl loud enough for her to hear.

See, I'm just hungry. "The consensus from my stomach and my brain is, yes, please."

"Come inside."

He followed her onto the porch, and apparently her cat thought it was a race because he darted past Jake and through the open doorway. His ex, aka Miss Velcro, had adopted a cat in both of their names after only a few weeks of dating. Proof she hadn't known him at all. There was so much more wrong with that than just her not even bothering to ask if he liked cats.

Jessica's open-concept living space had tons of natural light and a massive fireplace. He realized he'd expected her place to be a mess like she'd been on the roadside, but everything was organized and neat as a pin. Even the magazines were fanned out perfectly on the coffee table beside a crystal bowl of assorted rocks and shells.

"I can make coffee if you want some," she said.

"Got any milk?" Her soft laugh was musical.

Not annoying or high-pitched. Just beautiful like her smile.

"I sure do. Two glasses of milk coming up. And I promise to do my best not to spill it on you."

Again, he gave her points for being someone who could laugh and joke about themselves.

"Meow."

Jake froze and slowly looked down. The big orange cat was standing right between his feet.

Move along, cat. Please. Move. Now.

When his attempt at a silent Jedi mind command didn't work, he narrowed his eyes at the animal, who apparently took the attention to mean have a seat. The feline tilted his head back to stare up at Jake while twitching his tail back and forth, whacking each of his ankles in rhythm.

"You can sit on one of the bar stools if you want."

He jerked his gaze to Jessica and found her grinning while she studied the pair of them. "Thanks," he said but didn't dare move while the animal was between his feet.

"Oliver, come get a treat." She pulled something from a big ceramic jar on the counter.

The cat trotted over and took a seat in front of her like a trained dog might do.

Jessica held the treat above him. "High five."

To Jake's surprise, the cat stood on his hind legs and tapped the side of her hand with his paw before accepting the treat. "I had no idea you could teach a cat to do tricks like that."

"He's the only one I've ever had that will do stuff like this. Sometimes I call him puppy-cat."

Jake sat on one of the bar stools at the kitchen island. "I had a dog who did lots of tricks. He passed away several months ago." Jake's heart still ached when he thought about Scout. He took a bite of cookie and was tempted to moan. Warm and soft with gooey chocolate. Perfect.

"It's so hard to lose a pet." Jessica remained standing on the other side of the kitchen island and bit into her own cookie.

"Sometimes I almost call his name and expect him to meet me at the door or come running to the fence when I drive up."

"Believe it or not, I've never had a dog, but now that I live in the country, I'll probably get one."

"I can help you pick the right one to protect you." When her eyes narrowed into a slight scowl that was more cute than imposing, Jake barely held back a grin. There was something about his comment she did not like.

"I want one as a companion, not a guard dog."

Aha, she doesn't like me saying she needs protection.

Hopefully this meant she wasn't too needy or clingy and would willingly go along with his take-things-slow plan. And also keep things casual because he wouldn't be around for long. "I hope you'll excuse the insinuation. That's the police officer in me talking. I recently became a master trainer."

"Oh, wow. That's what you did in Dallas?"

"It is." He hated thinking about the promotion he'd had to pass up, but he'd get back to doing what he truly loved at some point, soon. "Maybe we can go look at puppies together." That was something friends might do, and it could be a good way to take things nice and slow.

"That would be great. Does Oak Hollow have a K9 unit?"

"No, we don't, and that's part of the problem." Unable to resist, he grabbed another cookie, then watched the cat cross the room. He relaxed when the animal settled on the couch.

"But you want to start one?"

"I've tried to talk them into it but haven't had any luck." When Jessica propped her arms on the counter with one hip cocked to the side, his senses tingled, and it was a struggle to stay on topic. "I'd have to buy my own dog. And it's not in Oak Hollow's budget to pay a master trainer salary."

A slow smile spread across her face before she ducked her head, and he could practically see some kind of plan forming. And for some reason, it made his nerves rattle like pebbles in a tin can.

On their walk to the barn, they continued their conversation about beloved pets. It didn't take long to agree that the barn was perfectly suitable to board three horses, just as they'd both known it would be.

Back out in the sunshine, he looked toward the river. "I hear there's good fishing in this area."

"My father thought so. You like to fish?"

"Definitely. But I don't get to do it as often as I'd like."

"You are welcome to fish here anytime. If you want," she added with a shy smile.

"I want," he said, just to see if he could make her blush so prettily again. And it worked.

"If you feel like walking to the river, I'll show you the best spot."

They changed directions and made their way down the hill. A rainbow of wildflowers was scattered across the open space, and she paused every so often to pick one. All the colors reminded him of the unusual shades of Jessica's hair each of those long-ago summers. His favorite had been the blue, chin-length style. As she bent to add a daisy to her bouquet, the sunlight brought out a touch of red in her brown hair. This was definitely his new favorite color and style, and he wanted to bury his hands in it and see if it was as silky and thick as it looked.

"I love the sound of running water," she said.

Her voice pulled him from memories and places it shouldn't be going, and he became aware of the gurgle of water rushing around rocks. "Me, too."

Jessica hopped over a narrow strip of water and out onto a big flat rock that extended into the flowing river. "If I open my window at night, I can hear it."

"Did you bring that turtle out here?"

"I took him back to the coy pond by the gazebo, but it's funny you should mention that because I decided to name this rock Turtle Island." They sat on the rock, and she slipped off her shoes and put her feet into the water. "It's colder than I remember. So, tell me the good places to eat. Other than the Acorn Café," she said with a laugh. "I'm too embarrassed to go back in there for a while."

"Don't be. Everyone who saw the coffee incident was happily entertained. And the coffee came out in the wash." He wanted to smack his forehead. *Why did I say that last part? I sound like someone's grandma.* He glanced her way, but she wasn't laughing.

"I'll think about eating there again."

"You should go back." An idea struck. If he offered to take her there as a friend, he could win the house paint bet, and slowly get to know her at the same time. "So… I'm wondering if you can help a friend out with a bet with his old man?" He made sure to emphasize the word *friend*.

Her eyes widened. "I think you better tell me about the bet before I say yes."

"Wise woman. It's really more of a challenge, and it could also help you return to the scene of the coffee crime accompanied by the victim and show people there are no hard feelings."

She tucked up her knees and wrapped her arms around them. "I can't wait to hear the rest of this."

"The first one of us to…" He hesitated, not wanting to use the word *date*. "Ask a woman out gets to pick the paint color for our house."

"Wow. It must be a very heated paint battle."

"It is. And if you're willing to have a meal with me at the Acorn, I won't have to live in a house the color of things found in a baby's diaper."

She threw back her head and laughed, the ends of her long hair touching the rock. "Before I agree to help you out, tell me the color you want to paint your house."

Her teasing expression and their conversation had relaxed him, and she was loosening up, as well. "Two shades of green."

"I approve of green and would be happy to help out a friend."

"Cool, thanks." He watched her take a few deep breaths, and she seemed to go into her own thoughts while tapping her fingers on her leg, her top teeth pressed into her lower lip.

"Speaking of helping out a friend, I could use some help myself," she said. "And it's considerably bigger than a meal together."

He motioned for her to continue, but his warning radar turned on.

"You know that I'm planning to open my own veterinary practice and eventually a wildlife rescue."

"Yes."

"My father left me some money and it's in a trust. I had planned to withdraw a large chunk to start my business, but there's an unexpected problem with getting the amount I need all at once." She looked down and cleared her throat.

He should've known she had a trust fund to be able to afford this ranch. He had no idea how he could help with this problem, because he certainly didn't have any money to lend her.

"I couldn't help overhearing you on the phone the

other day at the station. I actually heard you talking about how expensive dogs are and that you're helping your dad with medical bills. How is he, by the way?"

"He's doing much better."

"That's good."

The way she was jumping all over the place with her thoughts was confusing. And she seemed even more nervous than before. "So, we've established that we both need money," he said. "How can I help with that?"

"I might have a solution for both of us to get the money we need."

"Tell me," he said in a reluctant tone, unsure if he actually wanted to hear what would come out of her mouth next.

She met his eyes and swallowed a couple of times. "To get the money… I need to be married."

Alarm bells clanged along with his radar and every hair on his body rose to attention.

Oh, hell, no. Do not say what I think you are about to say.

"Would you consider…" She let out a quick breath.

Jake gripped the rock next to him hard enough to press painfully into his palm. *No! Don't ruin this by saying it.*

"This is a bigger ask than yours. Would you consider a marriage of convenience?" she said quickly and bit her lip again.

Jake was rarely speechless, but he was now. Bigger? Hell, this favor was enormous and pure crazy talk. Was she trying to win the clingy-woman crown?

There was a long silence before she waved her

hands as if shooing something away. "Never mind," she said and got to her feet. "It was a ridiculous thing to even consider."

There was something they could agree on. "Yeah, um…" He looked at his watch. "I should probably get home to check on my dad and cook dinner."

"Of course. I've kept you here too long. Please, don't tell anyone I even brought up this idea." After grabbing her shoes, she started for the house, still barefoot.

What was a guy supposed to make of this whammy of an unexpected proposition?

He sat there a moment longer, freaking out on the inside but determined to hide it. Just when he was having fun hanging out with her, she had to go and yank the rug out from under him. Once his game face was in place, he caught up to Jessica. If he casually played this off as no big deal, then he could make a run for it, and this topic could be buried and never talked about again.

Their dinner plans were better forgotten, and if he didn't bring it up again, hopefully she wouldn't, either. And that was disappointing because he had been looking forward to their date. Now he'd have to find a way to keep his distance, which would not be easy in this town. Especially if the horses were boarded out here.

But marrying a woman he barely knew was absolutely a no go. Period. The end.

On the drive home from Jessica's ranch, Jake kept replaying her shocking request to marry her.

For money. Wait until he told Anson about this. He would no doubt think Jake was making it up, and he wished that he was. He'd been looking forward to getting to know her.

When he got home, he found Pops sitting at the kitchen table frowning at a stack of papers with that look on his face. The one that said something was wrong. An unexpected weight pressed down on his shoulders. "What's happened?"

"A bill from the hospital."

"Another one?"

"This one is from the anesthesiologist."

Jake took a seat across from him and picked up the bill. His eyes widened. "Damn. You'd think your company would have better insurance coverage."

"I also got a call from the doctor. She wants me to start taking a new medication that the insurance won't cover. I asked her to see if there is another option, but she said there isn't one as good as this." Pops rubbed his hands over his cheeks. "I'll just tell her to give me the old medicine."

"No. You need to take the best one. We'll find a way."

"I'll have to go back to work sooner than planned."

"That doesn't sound like a good idea, either." Jake did not want him overdoing it too soon and ending up back in the hospital, or worse. A sharp chill grabbed hold of his spine.

"I already took out one loan against the house when all the plumbing had to be replaced. And I haven't even told you that we need a new roof, and it has to be the kind approved for historic homes, which is of course more expensive. As much as I hate to consider it, I think we need to talk about selling the house and getting something smaller and farther out of town."

Shock hit the pit of his stomach like lead weights. "Pops, don't say that. We won't have to sell the house." He knew how attached his dad was to the family home he'd inherited from his grandparents, because he was just as attached.

"What are you planning to do? Have one of us sell a kidney or something?"

He knew his dad was frustrated and upset, and he couldn't blame him. "No one is selling organs."

But he might need to consider selling his freedom to a woman with gorgeous brown eyes.

Chapter Seven

By the next morning, Jessica had baked three kinds of cookies and a peach pie, and blueberry muffins were currently baking. Her go-to stress activity was either going to fill up her freezer or make some new friends happy. Keeping her hands busy with baking had always helped her think through problems, and yesterday's conversation with Jake was requiring a lot of kitchen therapy. Maybe she could make extra money selling baked goods, but it would take a heck of a lot of cookies, cakes and muffins to earn what she needed to start a brand-new business.

After an almost sleepless night of thinking, she was starting to come to terms with her monetary issue and marital situation. Sort of. She replayed their riverside conversation and groaned.

"What was I thinking? It's w-a-a-ay too soon to ask him something like that," she said to her cat as he skidded around the corner of the kitchen island after his favorite bouncy ball. "And Jake left without picking a time for our dinner date. Guess our meal at the Acorn is off the table. He'd rather paint his house the colors of poo than hang out with the wacky woman who proposed marriage after a few days."

Oliver circled her feet and wrapped his tail around her ankle as if knowing she needed comfort. At least she was no worse off than where she was before suggesting a fake marriage. If you didn't count the sudden tension with Jake.

"Maybe I should bake some nut-free banana bread for the police station."

The timer rang and she was pulling muffins from the oven when the sound of gravel under tires alerted her to someone's arrival, but she wasn't expecting anyone. From her spot in the kitchen, there was a clear view of her circular drive, and she blinked to confirm the scene.

Jake is here?

Well, wasn't this the surprise of the day, and it wasn't even nine o'clock. What did it mean that he'd come back only hours later? Her thoughts started bouncing around like Oliver's ball, but she needed to hold off on making any assumptions. Before he even made it onto the porch, she opened the front door. "Good morning."

Taking one hand out of the front pocket of his faded jeans, he waved. "Morning."

When his eyes dipped low, then widened before staring at a spot above her head, she remembered what she was wearing. Pink-and-white sleep shorts with a matching unicorn-print tank top. And no bra. His reaction was too entertaining to feel embarrassed, but she did cross her arms over her breasts.

"I should've called first." He took a step back.

"It's okay. Come in. I just took blueberry muffins out of the oven."

"I have good timing." Jake came up the steps and they shared an awkward smile. "So far I'm two for two when it comes to arriving while you're baking."

"Would you like coffee or milk?" she asked over her shoulder on her way to the kitchen.

"Coffee, please. Always coffee in the mornings."

"Good answer."

Is it possible he's even more handsome than yesterday?

She was overheating, and it wasn't because she was standing near the oven. The man was handsome in his uniform, but in jeans and a maroon T-shirt stretched around and defining his muscles, he was more delicious than the treats she'd been baking. Jessica grabbed the apron she'd been wearing, pulled it over her head and tied it behind her back. It would at least provide some degree of modesty.

"I have to say, I'm surprised to see you back out here."

"I'm a bit surprised myself." His eyes scanned the array of baked goods on her marble countertop. "Are you having a bake sale?"

"No. I just got a little carried away. I'll pack some up for you to take home."

"Thanks." He took a seat on one of the stools at the island and propped his forearms on the marble surface. "Do you have time to talk?"

"Sure." Her pulse raced as if she'd run a marathon. "What's up?" She placed a cup of coffee and the cream and sugar in front of him.

"You're getting good at serving drinks without spilling them on me."

"Very funny." The warmth of a blush spread across her face, but his smile made her whole body heat up.

"So…" He paused and added cream to his cup. "I'm sorry I rushed away like I did last night."

That's why he's here. To apologize.

Standing on the opposite side of the island, she put a warm muffin on a plate and slid it his way. "I don't blame you at all. It was ridiculous of me to even ask something like that. I should apologize for putting you in an awkward situation."

"I did kind of open up the conversation by asking you to help me win the house paint bet." Jake took a bite, chewed and made a satisfied sound. "I thought maybe we could discuss it a little more?"

Her heart gave an extra-strong thump against her breastbone. "Really? Wait. I want to make sure we're talking about the same thing. Are you talking about the date to win the challenge with your dad or…the other?"

"The other," he said quickly, then dipped his chin and took another bite.

"Oh. Wow. Okay." Apparently, she was capable of only one-word sentences.

"You're wanting to do this to get access to the money to start your business? And that's the *only* reason?"

Her muscles tensed. His extra emphasis of the word *only* was a sharp reminder. Her only mission was her ranch and veterinary practice, but somehow she'd allowed his blue eyes and sexy smile to subliminally slip a new desire into her brain.

"Yes. Of course that's the only reason," she said. "This situation arose so suddenly my head was spinning. I only found out about the trust fund condition the day after I moved in. I started to look for a job, and as you so unfortunately know, that didn't go so well. Then when I heard you say you needed money, too, the idea just popped into my head."

"Makes sense. I can understand that."

"But I should've just kept my mouth shut and started saving up each month. Delaying my plans isn't the end of the world by any means."

He studied her and sipped his coffee. "Knowing you as a teenager, I never would have guessed you were a trust fund kid. You never…you know, acted entitled or better than anyone."

"Well, that's good to hear." She was glad to know he didn't think she was a spoiled brat, because expecting everything she wanted to come easily was making her feel like one.

"I've been going over reasons for and against your idea," he said. "Would it be like a planned-out agreement between friends? And would the real reason for the marriage be kept a secret from everyone else?"

"Definitely a secret." She tapped a fingertip on her lips, unable to believe this conversation was happening. "A mutually beneficial arrangement between us, but to everyone else it would look like a real marriage."

"Right. No one else would need to know we're only two friends helping one another out."

Wow, he's really driving home the friends *part of it. But at least he's considering it.* "Exactly. A secret arrangement between friends."

"Here's the thing." He sucked in a quick breath and froze, his eyes the only body part to move as they cut downward.

"What's wrong?" She hurried around the kitchen island and saw Oliver with both front paws against Jake's knee. "Are you…allergic?"

"No-o-o." Drawing out the word, he never took his eyes off Oliver. "Had a bloody experience with a cat. My blood. Not the cat's."

"Ollie, come get a treat." Her pet performed his high-five trick, then wandered over to a sunny spot by the windows.

Jake visibly relaxed. "We both end up with treats when I come over."

"See, you're already finding things in common. You could be great friends and help one another out." She grinned at his one arched eyebrow expression.

"He's a sweet boy and won't hurt you. So, what were you about to say?"

"I would not feel right about just taking money from you like you're paying me as an escort or something."

"Oh, my goodness, no. I'm not implying that at all." *Although sharing his bed isn't the worst idea I've ever heard.*

"If we do this, I want to pay you back. Could we maybe make it a loan that I can pay back over time? You could even charge me interest."

"I hadn't expected for you to pay it back at all, but whatever makes you comfortable is fine with me. But being a part of this whole...charade would be worth more than interest on the money."

"I don't want anyone, not even my dad, to know it's about money."

"If you pay off medical bills, how will you keep it a secret?"

"I haven't gotten that far in the planning yet. Maybe tell him I worked out a deal with the insurance or hospital." He stood and eyed the cat before moving to the sink to wash his hands. "This is a situation I never in a million years thought I'd find myself even considering. You have an extra bedroom, right?"

This question made it clear that he did not plan to share a bedroom with her. "I have two extras.

"Are there ground rules for something like this?"

Jessica chuckled and handed him a clean hand

towel. "Your guess is as good as mine. Coming up with some guidelines isn't a bad idea."

"The way I see it, there are a few reasons to consider this… What did you call it?"

"A charade."

"You could start your practice and I could pay bills, help my dad and maybe even get a puppy to train. And as for me, everyone has been driving me crazy trying to set me up, and since I am not looking for a relationship, the way I figure it, if we do this it will get everyone off my back."

Not looking for a relationship. Got it.

He picked up his mug of coffee. "But I might be getting ahead of myself. I haven't even asked what kind of money you're talking about."

"Would $250,000 be enough to start?"

He almost choked on his sip of coffee and started coughing. "To start?" His voice was higher pitched than normal, and he cleared his throat and tried again. "That's more than I had thought. It would take me a long time to pay that back."

"It can be however much you're comfortable with, and you can take all the time you need, because like I said, I had not expected you to pay any of it back."

"I could also help you out around the ranch. You said you'd like another corral built off the side of your barn. I'm good with my hands."

"Good to know. My barn would appreciate some attention." She couldn't resist teasing him. If they couldn't be playful, this would never work.

His eyes widened before his grin spread wide.

"So, how can we do this in a short amount of time without everyone whispering behind our backs?" she asked.

His laugh made Oliver raise his head. "You've never lived in a small town, have you? Folks will whisper no matter what."

"Oh. How long do you think people will consider too quick to be married?"

"No idea."

"I guess we could claim love at first sight?" The warmth of a blush crept up her neck and she busied herself with wiping the already clean countertop. "Or something else."

He tugged the collar of his T-shirt. "We could start with the date at the Acorn Café, like we already had planned. It's the place to go if we want to be seen by enough—and the right—people. Word will spread like wildfire. We have a lot of well-meaning but nosy folks in Oak Hollow."

She pulled a blank recipe card from her open file box and jotted down a few guidelines while saying them aloud.

1. Be seen together and get people talking.

2. Agreement between friends.

3. Money is a loan with no interest.

4. Separate bedrooms.

She'd added number four because not sharing a room seemed to be one of his concerns, and it did set some boundaries ahead of time. "Then a few more dates and after a certain amount of time…we could elope?" she asked.

"Yeah. Eloping is really the only option. We can go to the courthouse in San Antonio."

Meaning…there would not be a real wedding. That fact made an ache build inside her, because this could be her only marriage, fake or not. She was surprised to realize that a part of her actually wanted to don a white dress and toss a bouquet. "I'll add eloping to San Antonio to the list. I've never been there, but I've heard it's a fun place."

"Guess we could turn it into a weekend trip." He met and held her gaze. "Just so you'd have time to see some of the town. Most hotel rooms have two beds. Or we could get separate rooms."

Message received. Not a honeymoon.

She turned the card around and put it in front of him. "I'm agreeable to this if you are. I'm sure we will think of more things that need to be added. But you should look it over and make changes and additions. Then we can discuss."

Jake picked up the card. "Should we add the part about keeping it a secret?"

"Yes. Definitely." How had she forgotten to add that part? "This is a big secret but absolutely necessary to keep private."

"You seem very concerned about anyone finding out."

"I am." She didn't know all the details her father had written into the trust but questioning or discussing it with Aunt Kay would tip her off. "The marriage has to appear real to gain access to the extra funds."

"That makes sense."

"Plus, not long ago, I was publicly humiliated by a boyfriend. And I don't want to go through something like that again."

"That sucks. What happened?" He held up his hands. "Sorry. Too soon to ask stuff that personal."

She tended to agree and stopped herself before revealing anything that might send him running. "One thing I will say is, he told me I was the kind of woman you date, but not the marrying kind."

Jake's face scrunched. "The marrying kind? What's that mean?"

"Exactly what I asked him. Apparently, in his mind, a wife should not be so career oriented because that doesn't leave enough time to take care of him and his home. I told him the 1950s called and wanted their attitude back."

"Good answer." Jake held up the recipe card. "Can I take this with me? I need to go help someone move furniture."

"Sure. Just please don't show it to anyone or lose it. Let me pack up a few things for you and your dad." Grabbing a large plastic container, Jessica loaded it with cookies and muffins.

"We might as well get started on this plan," he said and put the recipe card into his back pocket. "Are you free for dinner tonight?"

"I am."

"I can pick you up at six and we can arrive together. Sound okay?"

"Works for me." She walked him to the door, and

when he stuck out his hand for a shake, she accepted. His skin was warm and sent a tingle up her arm, but the formality of it was more confirmation that this would be nothing more than a marriage of convenience. A business agreement. With no added benefits, other than money.

As soon as his truck was out of sight, Jessica sagged onto the couch. "What just happened?" One of her grandmother's expressions popped into her head.

You've gotten yourself into a real pickle, missy.

And now she felt the need to bake cupcakes.

Chapter Eight

"Why are you so dressed up?" Pops asked on the way to his favorite chair with a glass of iced tea and a book.

Jake looked down at his clothes. Nice jeans, boots and a blue button-up weren't that dressed up. "I don't know what you're talking about. I wear these clothes all the time."

"I call bull on that."

"You got me." Jake let his grin grow wide and shoved his wallet into his back pocket. "Tomorrow I'll go buy green paint for the house."

"What? You have a date?" Pops tried to look affronted but couldn't hide his underlying amusement and satisfaction.

"Yes, I do."

"With who?"

"Jessica Talbot. The new veterinarian, and the one who was changing a tire on the side of the road."

His dad's eyebrows settled back into place as he smiled. "Thought you weren't attracted to her."

Jake shrugged. "I've decided I'm going to be less like Mom and give people a chance before judging or jumping to conclusions."

Pops made a noise in his throat. "That woman is definitely judgy, but sometimes I miss her."

He misses her?

That was a statement he'd never heard Pops say, but he had noticed and wondered about his parents talking and spending more time together when she came to town.

A few feet inside of Jessica's front gate, Jake stopped his truck. He'd be a few minutes late picking her up for their first date, but his stomach had decided to twist into a knot. He was tempted to turn around and forget this whole thing, but he couldn't. Not when he'd already agreed to do this. Not when Pops was considering selling the family home they loved. A home Jake thought he'd inherit and be the fifth generation of Carters to own it.

A minute or two was all he needed to get his head in the right place, because he knew what he had to do. He'd approached this marriage like a job. They could have a professional relationship. A friendship. Like the undercover spy couple in the movie he'd watched with Pops. Jake laughed and rested his head on the top of the steering wheel. He was no actor. More than one person had laughed at his skills in his mandatory high school drama class.

Replaying the ideas he and Jessica had discussed that morning, he pulled the recipe card from his shirt pocket. It had a row of cupcakes decorating the top and a list of things that would alter his world written right there in black-and-white. Front and back.

He was doing this for his dad. For their family home. He could get a dog before returning to Dallas and doing something about his old truck wouldn't be a bad idea. And he could help Jessica start her veterinary practice.

When he finally made it to her front door, she answered with a bright smile, and he marveled once more at the difference between now and their first meeting. Her flower-print sundress showed off graceful shoulders, and he barely resisted touching her to see if her skin was as soft as it looked. There was no hiding her beauty tonight. "You look very nice."

"Thanks, you, too. But you always do."

He stepped back and motioned to his truck. "Are you ready?"

"I am." After grabbing a purse from the small table by the door, she stepped out and locked up before following him toward his truck.

Was he supposed to open her door like it was a real date, or treat her like a buddy? In his moment of indecision, she was already climbing up into his tall truck. And with her long legs, she had no problem. The ride into town was filled with stretches of silence, but it wasn't as uncomfortable as one might think. He pointed out things as they drove like a tour guide, and she talked about summers spent in Oak Hollow.

He found a parking spot across from the Acorn, and unable to ignore his mother's lessons about being a Southern gentleman, Jake hurried to her side and helped her down. Her sweet smile told him she appreciated the gesture. So he also held the door of the Acorn Café, then followed her inside.

Like a synchronized dance, the people facing them whispered to their companions who turned to look—some more obvious than others. He inwardly groaned. They'd be this evening's topic of conversation. But as uncomfortable as that made him, that *was* the whole reason they were here. It was step one of their charade.

He led her to an empty booth right in the middle of the café. Trying to be seen was an instant success. Three people came over to say hello before they even had their drinks.

Jessica laid her hand over his on the tabletop. "Touching one another is sure to get all the Gladys Kravitz types talking."

"The what?"

"I guess you've never watched *Bewitched*? Samantha the good witch who twitches her nose to do magic?" She hummed the theme song.

"Oh, that old sitcom. My grandmother used to watch it on the retro channel. But who's Gladys Kravitz?"

"She was the quintessential nosy neighbor who was into everyone else's business."

He laughed. "Got it. There are several Oak Hollow versions of her." When her fingers flexed, he realized he was still holding her hand. It felt so natural he'd laced their fingers without realizing what he'd done.

"What's up?" asked a man's familiar voice.

Jake slipped his hand from Jessica's and turned to meet Luke Walker's grin. "Showing our newest citizen around town. You remember Jessica?"

"I sure do. Nice to see you again."

"You, too. And I'm proud to report that I haven't caused Jake a bit of trouble this evening."

"The night is still young," Jake said, then held his breath. It was probably too soon for that kind of joking around.

Her pursed lips lifted into a mischievous grin that accentuated her high cheekbones. "Where's a hot cup of coffee when you need it?" Jessica made a motion like she was pouring something on him.

Jake relaxed, once again appreciating her playfulness. "Good one."

His buddy chuckled. "You're going to get along so well with my wife."

"Are you talking about me again?" Alexandra asked as she walked up behind him.

"I sure am."

"Jessica and I have already met and bonded over dessert at book club." Alexandra glanced over her shoulder. "This is our son, Cody."

The little boy peeked out from behind her.

"Hi, Cody." Jessica waved to him.

Cody pointed to the menu that was propped in a

metal stand behind the salt and pepper. "Momma Alex painted that tree," he whispered and then ducked back into his hiding place.

"Oh, wow, Alexandra," Jessica said. "You really are a talented artist."

"Thanks. I enjoy it. I painted that tree of life with watercolors while I was sitting at the counter right over there."

"We'll let y'all get back to your date," Luke said in his slight Southern drawl.

Jake started to tell them it wasn't a real date, but clamped his mouth shut. This *was* a date. At least it was supposed to appear that way. And…it felt that way.

Oh, hell. I'm off to a terrible start.

Treating this arrangement like a job was going to be more challenging than the police academy.

Jessica let her gaze follow the other couple. They'd held hands from the moment Alexandra stepped up beside Luke until they were seated. How amazing it must feel to have that kind of love. The butterflies had danced in her belly when Jake held her hand across the table, but that had only been an act. She pressed a hand to her racing heart. What if going through with this plan meant she'd miss meeting her true love? What if she kept Jake from meeting his?

It's utterly absurd that I'm considering marriage when there's no love between us.

And she couldn't forget one of her very important rules. Never get involved with a man who has a dangerous job. Too many threats and bad people were waiting to break hearts and ruin lives, just like the man who'd killed her father while he protected a celebrity.

"Jessica? Jess?"

She met Jake's concerned gaze across the table. "Sorry. What did you say?"

"Will you be okay if I go talk to someone real quick?"

"Of course." She let her gaze follow him across the café. He'd been attractive as a teen, but now, Jake Carter was masculine, handsome and caring, and he gave her all those tingly feelings a girl looks for. *How am I supposed to have a fake relationship with someone I'm so attracted to?*

This whole thing was a mistake. She'd have to find a way to tell him she'd been too hasty, and they should not go through with this marriage of convenience. The best thing for both of them would be to stop this crazy train she'd let out of the station.

Jake returned as the waiter arrived with their orders. "Sorry about that interruption. I wanted to thank someone for bringing food to my dad."

"How is he?" she asked while adding ketchup to her fries and trying to think of a way to tell him she'd changed her mind.

"Healing, but he needs a couple of new medications. Expensive ones." He met her gaze. "My dad is considering selling our house, and I can't let that happen. It's been a family home since my great-grandparents built it in 1916."

Jessica stomach dropped to her toes. *Oh, shoot.*

His eyes told the story of a man dedicated to his family. There was no backing out of this now. "I'm glad I can help you." And it was true, but this was going to be harder than her attempt at becoming a ballerina. "We haven't talked about how long we will… play this thing out," she whispered.

"I thought about when it should come to an end. I made some notes." He pulled the recipe card from his pocket and slid it across the table. It had writing in a second color of ink that continued onto the back side. "But I guess we can't really talk about this here."

"No. Not a good idea." With another quick glance at the recipe card, she slipped it into her purse. "We can discuss it on the way home."

Reminding herself why she'd started this whole thing, she took a deep breath and ate a French fry. Going through with this would allow her access to the funds to start her practice and keep her ranch without a monthly struggle to make the payments. It would help Jake and his father. And at least she wouldn't have the issue of Jake telling her that she couldn't keep a man happy long-term.

They'd go into this charade knowing it had an end date.

She wasn't sure if she was relieved or sad that he'd thought about when to end their marriage of convenience.

After enjoying some good food and being the topic of conversation, they walked around the square. People came and went from the café, a couple of shops and Sip & Read. Others seemed to be taking evening walks as they passed by or went into the ice cream shop. The small businesses appeared to be thriving, but compared to the crowds Jessica was used to in Los Angeles, the square was a low-key Saturday night.

Once they were in his truck and headed back to her ranch, she pulled the card from her purse. He'd written *Recipe for a Fake Marriage* under the row of dancing cupcakes. "Clever title."

"It just popped into my head. Probably because you're always baking for me."

An image of them baking together like a real couple made her heart speed. What would Mr. Clean do if she threw flour on him? To keep from leaning across the truck's center console and touching him, she forced herself to look at the card in her hand.

He'd added: *Keep this a secret, More fake dates* and *End date?*

"So, how many dates do you think is enough before eloping?"

"Hard to say, but with as much pressure as I'm getting from people who think of themselves as matchmakers, I don't expect negative reactions from anyone." He rubbed the back of his neck. "At least I don't think there will be."

"No women trying to catch your attention that I might need to fight off?" Her stomach tightened into a weird knot. Had that question sounded too... jealous? Because she wasn't. Not at all.

Keep telling yourself that, Jess.

Jake cleared his throat. "Might be one or two, but no one that I would consider dating."

"Why don't we wait and see how people react? Play it by ear for now?"

"Works for me," he said. "There's a band playing at a new venue on Wednesday evening. That would be a good second date. Lots of people. And what do you think about me spending some time fishing on your ranch tomorrow? That way my dad will see things developing. Or I could help you get some work done instead."

"I think fishing is a great plan. There is no work that's urgent. Not until I can start building my clinic." Feeling overheated at the thought of spending more time with him, she directed an air conditioner vent her way. "I had a thought about your dad. Since he's still healing, will he need to live with us?"

"No. He'll be fine. I've just been there to keep him from overdoing it too soon. And since he can't know it's a fake marriage, he can't be there to see us sleeping in different bedrooms."

The words *fake marriage* made her wince but hearing how resolute he was about separate bedrooms stung even more. But not sleeping together was a good thing. A romance was not her focus. She shifted in her seat and adjusted the seat belt strap that suddenly seemed to be compressing her chest. Or maybe that was just her conscience. "That brings us back to the question of when and how to end our…agreement."

"I have the perfect reason for how and why. I

probably should have mentioned this earlier," Jake said and glanced her way briefly. "Not many people know this yet, but I have a job offer with my old K9 unit in Dallas. It's not a huge promotion but a good start, and I'll get to work with dogs again."

He's leaving town?

Heaviness settled in her limbs. "Oh. Wow. That's great," she said with as much excitement as she could muster. "When do you start your new job?"

"That's why I put a question mark beside the end date on the recipe card. I'm not sure yet. But not before Pops gets an all clear to return to work, and I can see that he's listening to the doctors and not overdoing it like he used to." Jake changed the radio station. "Anyway, it's a lot more money than I make here and will allow me to pay you back more quickly. And since Oak Hollow isn't starting a K9 unit here, I can't do what I love if I stay."

Although she was bummed that he didn't plan to stay in Oak Hollow, living in the same small town after their breakup could be problematic. And long-distance relationships never worked, which was an additional reason not to have a "real" relationship. This way it would be a clean break. *And the way I'm falling, probably heartbreak on my end.*

"It's what I've wanted to do since I was a little kid," he said. "I was about to get the promotion when Pops had his heart attack, but luckily they're holding a position for me."

"You're a very good son for coming home to take care of your dad."

"I try."

Jake had given up a promotion, and his reason was honorable, but she'd given up a job she'd really wanted for a stupid guy who'd never loved her. That had just been poor decision making on her part.

"Please tell me we won't need to have a public breakup fight." he said. "Because I'm not a good actor."

"No." Jessica shivered. "That kind of thing is one of my fears. I might be from Hollywood, but I'm no actor, either. I definitely do *not* want a public breakup scene. Especially in a small town where I want to become a respected citizen."

Jake made a noise of agreement and pulled to a stop in front of her cabin. "How are we supposed to pull off this charade if neither of us can act?"

"Excellent question. Want to come in for a piece of pie and we can hammer this plan out?"

"You had me at pie."

His grin took her breath.

And you had me when we fell into the bluebonnets.

Chapter Nine

Jake got up before sunrise, left his dad a note and took his fishing gear out to Jessica's ranch. When he got out of his truck, the night crickets still chirped, and not wanting to wake her, either, he made his way to the big flat rock she'd named Turtle Island. It was a perfect place to set up and fish.

Facing the rising sun, he stood perfectly still and closed his eyes, waiting for that brief, almost elusive moment of silence separating night from day. He opened his eyes with the birdsong, and the sunrise wasn't the only thing of beauty to admire. Cast in silhouette by golden morning light, her face was in shadows, and she was his mystery woman once again. A few more steps and her shy smile came into view.

She's so beautiful and...

Warmth started in his chest and spread. There was something he couldn't put a finger on. Something about her that called to him.

Her cut-off denim shorts showed off tanned legs at least a mile long. The world was waking up, and so was his libido. Being a bad actor in front of everyone was going to be nothing compared to the skills it would take when they were alone. The struggle would be keeping his desires a secret. Starting right now.

He returned her wave. "Good morning. Hope I didn't wake you when I drove up?"

"No. Oliver took care of that. And I'm an early riser." Jessica held up a wicker picnic basket. "I brought a thermos of coffee and banana bread muffins without any nuts at all."

"I'll have to run ten extra miles a week with all of your baking, but that doesn't mean I won't have some of both." His mouth was already watering at the thought of biting into the banana bread. "Do you cook regular food, too?"

"I do." She sat cross-legged on the rock beside his gear and opened the basket. "What about you?"

"Does Hamburger Helper, frozen dinners and barbecue count?"

"Hmm." While opening the thermos, she pretended to give it deep thought, then grinned and poured a cup. "Well… I suppose it does."

The aroma of coffee mixed with the fresh herbal scent of grass still damp from morning dew, and the metal cup was warm against his hand.

She handed him a muffin on a napkin. "Will it mess up your fishing if I put my feet in the water?"

"Not if you're still and don't splash around."

Shoes kicked off, she eased her legs into the clear water and sucked in a quick breath. "This spring-fed river feels so cold at first. Especially this early in the morning before the sun has heated things up."

"Seventy-two degrees, all year long." Jake loved fishing and spending time in nature, and Jessica was turning out to be good company. They talked now and then but were able to sit in silence and it wasn't uncomfortable.

As the sun rose higher, something shimmered as it moved through the water, then stuck on a pointed rock.

Jessica shielded her eyes with her hand. "What is that shiny silver thing out there?"

"I can't tell."

She stood and, after testing her balance, walked out into the thigh-high water until she reached the rock. The hem of her cutoffs grew darker as water wicked into the faded denim. "It's a deflated Mylar balloon." She pulled it free and unfolded it. "It says congratulations on your engagement."

She turned to him with the cutest wide-eyed expression, and they stared at one another for a moment before bursting into laughter.

"Should we take that as a sign that we're doing the right thing?" he asked.

"I think so. The universe is sending us a message." On her way back to the riverbank, she gasped as her arms windmilled, the balloon flapping like a flag. In the next moment, she slipped sideways into the water with a splash sure to scare every fish around.

Her head popped out of the water, and he knew she wasn't hurt, but at the same time he was already in the river on his way to help her up. Jake didn't even try to hold back his laughter, especially when she squealed and declared the spring-fed river had to be colder than seventy-two degrees.

Wiping wet hair from her face, and still holding the balloon in her other hand, she shot him a crooked grin. "You think this is funny?"

"Yep. I sure do."

"Help me up."

When he took her outstretched hand, she threw herself backward and pulled him all the way into the water.

"Now who's laughing?" She splashed him.

They both were. And he was enjoying himself more than he had in a long while.

"Oh, no, I dropped our sign from the universe." Pushing off the rocky river bottom, she propelled herself forward and grabbed the balloon. "The water feels nice once you get used to it. Could you put this by the picnic basket, please?"

He took the deflated balloon, walked the few steps back to Turtle Island and laid it out to dry beside the basket.

"It gets deeper over here," she said.

Rather than getting out of the water, he followed

her into a deeper part of the river. "Good thing I put on cargo shorts instead of jeans. They'll dry quicker."

"It was very chivalrous of you to get your clothes wet coming to my rescue, even if you were laughing."

"It's in my nature." The water's current pushed her close enough that their arms touched. His body warmed in response, but when the length of her bare leg brushed against his, his temperature spiked. He was suddenly very thankful for the cold water.

"You still have on your tennis shoes," she said.

"Yep." He wiggled his toes, wondering how long it would take them to dry. "Didn't really have time to take them off."

"Sorry about that," she said and started to move away from him.

"Wait." He stepped forward to pull a leaf from her hair right as she turned back, and they came face-to-face. Her wet skin glistened, and tiny drops of water clung to her lips. When he reached for the leaf, she sucked in a breath and her pupils dilated. Was she expecting a kiss? It would be so easy to move just a little closer and press his mouth to hers.

Don't do it, dude.

"A leaf. In your hair." He was having trouble forming words. Which meant he was going to have even more trouble being a fake husband.

"Oh. Thanks." Her voice was breathy and huskier than normal.

When she grabbed the hem of her T-shirt, he was the one catching his breath. Worried she'd gotten the wrong idea, he intended to protest, but his mouth still refused to cooperate. As her shirt came off, relief fought with disappointment at the sight of a pink bikini top.

Jessica tossed her wet T-shirt and it landed with a splat beside the balloon. "I wore a swimsuit just in case this kind of thing happened. And I don't want to get a farmer's tan."

"I should've done the same."

And I should've stayed out of the water. Or better yet, stayed home.

Also not wanting a white chest and back from a T-shirt tan, he took off his own wet shirt and tossed it beside hers. He heard her gasp and say, "Wow," but when he turned around, she was looking at the sky. It was only his wishful thinking that her exclamation was for him.

With her face tipped up to the sun, her dark hair floated around her bare shoulders, and he could so easily imagine untying the string of her bikini top and pulling her against his chest.

"I think I probably scared all the fish away."

"More will come along," he said. Suddenly, fishing didn't seem so important.

They hung out in an area where the water came up to mid chest and eased into a conversation about the things she wanted to do around the ranch.

"I'm already hungry. Are you?" she asked.

"I can almost always eat."

She started for Turtle Island. "I have stuff to make sandwiches up at the cabin."

"Sounds good."

Jessica gasped, her back colliding with his chest and doing nothing to ease his urge to hold her. Which was exactly what he was doing now. She was in his arms, her head tipped back enough that their cheeks brushed, and the heat of her body sent a shiver across his skin.

"Are you okay" he asked.

"I stepped on something sharp." She braced her hands on his forearms and lifted one foot, causing her to press back against him even more as if she had complete trust in his support. "It's fine. No blood."

He kept his arms around her and moved toward Turtle Island. Her slightly injured foot seemed like a good enough excuse to keep touching her.

On their walk to her house, she veered off the straightest path to stand in the circle of shade provided by a huge oak tree sitting all alone in the open space between the river and her cabin. "I'd like to put a bench under Granddaddy Oak."

"Is that an official tree term," he teased.

"No." She smiled. "It's just the name that came to me years ago when I first saw it. It's so big and majestic and seems to be watching over everything. I used to sit under it and read every summer that we vacationed here." She picked up a small rock, rolled it around in her hand and then slipped it into her pocket. "I could hang some bird feeders and add a birdbath. Turn the area into an awesome hangout spot."

"That sounds pretty easy to accomplish. I can help you."

"I'd appreciate that."

"I can build the bench."

She was ahead of him as they continued walking, but she got so excited she turned around and walked backward. "Oh, a hammock or one of those hammock chairs that hangs from a branch."

"That's totally doable. Thanks for letting me hang out today."

"Any time. I think today has shown us that we can be friends and work together to make people believe we're a real couple."

Right. Friends. Fake relationship. Slow and cautious like a turtle.

On Monday morning, Jessica started her car and automatically prepared herself for the stress of jammed-up traffic. *Wait a minute.* Just as quickly, relief made her laugh. She'd likely drive all the way to the center of town with barely a slowdown.

Another step in their Recipe for a Fake Marriage was for her to be seen visiting Jake at the police station. This was the first time she'd willingly become a topic of gossip, but they needed to keep the rumor train rolling.

But on her way across the street with her shopping bag of baked goodies, the butterflies in her belly tugged her toward the door of Tess's antique store instead. She just needed another minute or so to ready herself to see her "friend" Jake. Jessica entered the store and was greeted by an adorable little girl. Down syndrome gave her beautiful blue eyes a unique shape and her curly blond pigtails bounced as she danced around a table.

She stopped dancing, swished the full skirt of her dress and waved. "Hi. You a pretty lady."

"Thank you. You're very pretty, too. I'm Jessica, and you must be Hannah."

"Hannah Lynn Curry." She gave a little hop after each word. "My daddy the chief." The little girl's smile was beaming with pride and love. She turned to Tess, who walked up beside her. "Momma, a costume here."

Tess chuckled and adjusted one of Hannah's pigtails. "Customer." She turned her dimpled smile to Jessica. "I see you've met our store greeter."

"I sure have. Hannah is very good at her job."

"Tank you," the little girl said and walked a circle around both of them.

"I don't usually have her here with me, but today is a teacher's workshop day. I'm so glad you decided to stop by." Tess motioned for her to follow. "After our conversation at book club, I pulled out a few pieces of furniture I thought you might like."

"Oh, good. I can't wait to see what you have."

Hannah kept her eye on the bag of goodies Jessica carried as she trailed along beside them. When Jessica set the bag down, Hannah peered inside and sniffed. "You got cookies?"

"I sure do."

"Chockit chip?"

The child's hopeful expression made Jessica smile. "Yes." She glanced at Tess, who nodded confirmation that her daughter could have a cookie. "Would you like one?"

"Yes, peas." The little cutie sat cross-legged on the shiny wooden floor and accepted her treat. "Tank you."

Jessica turned her attention to the items Tess had set aside for her. "This shelf is perfect for my bedroom."

"You like baby animals?" Hannah asked.

"I love them," Jessica said. "I'm a doctor for animals."

Hannah gasped and then grabbed Jessica's hand. "We go see babies."

"Oh, I don't have any baby animals right now."

The little girl tugged her hand. "Daddy has babies."

Jessica once again turned to Tess for clarification, but instead caught the other woman's unmistakable sadness as she pressed a hand to her flat belly.

They must be trying to have a baby.

She wanted to hug her new friend and tell her everything would be okay, but that would only be pretty words. There was never a guarantee for anything in life, and the Talbot family knew that well enough. Her father always told her not to worry about his going to work. But he'd been killed while protecting a celebrity client. And Emma… She'd breezed through an easy pregnancy only to lose her baby and husband in a senseless accident.

"Daddy has two babies." Hannah held up one finger on each hand.

Tess's hand dropped from her stomach, and she smiled. "A neighbor brought over two baby raccoons this morning, and they're in Anson's office next door."

"Well, in that case, I think the furniture can wait." Jessica picked up her bag of baked goods. "Let's go see the kits."

"What's kits?" the little girl asked.

"That's what you call a baby raccoon. Kind of like a baby dog is a puppy and a baby cat is called a kitten."

"Hannah loves animals and even thinks bugs are cute," Tess said as they walked next door to the police station. "Please, tell my husband I'll come get her in a few minutes. I have to wait for my employee to arrive."

"I'll tell him."

When Jessica and Hannah walked into the station, Jake was nowhere in sight, but Anson was in his back corner office behind walls that were mostly glass. Not very private but probably provided a sound barrier. If Jake had been in there, she never would've heard him saying he needed money, and they wouldn't be planning their marriage of convenience.

The police chief saw them and came out of his office just in time to catch his daughter's flying leap. "How's my little one?"

"Daddy, show the babies," she whispered like it was a special secret.

"Are you taking in wildlife yet?" Anson asked.

"I can. I have all of the permits and licensing in place." Chittering that sounded similar to chirping birds led her to a cardboard box behind his desk. It was lined with towels and two kits were snuggled together. "Hello, you little cuties."

Hannah kneeled beside the box. "So cute." She giggled.

"How old do you think they are?" Anson asked.

Jessica gently picked up one of the baby raccoons and it was small enough to hold with one hand, his little feet clinging to her fingers. "Well, their eyes are open, but their teeth aren't in, so I'd say they are about four weeks."

"I guess they need to be bottle-fed?" he asked and kept Hannah from picking up the other kit.

"Yes, but they can't have cow's milk and will need a special milk replacement."

"And you are okay with taking them?"

"I sure am. It's not legal to have a pet raccoon in Texas, but I'll take care of them and then release them on my ranch once they are old enough."

As she was leaving with the box of raccoons, Jake came through the door, and the smile he gave her made her heart flutter.

"What do you have? Muffins or another turtle?" His eyes widened when chittering came from the box. "It's not baked goods."

"Nope. But I did leave a bag of goodies in the kitchen." She put the box on a chair and opened the lid. "Two raccoon kits. I'm going to take these little guys to work with me. I'm sure Doc Ty has what we will need to look after them."

"What is your cat going to think about them?"

"Oliver is a rescue with an unusual background. When he was a kitten, he lived with a litter of puppies about his age and a squirrel."

Jake brushed a finger over one of their little head. "So, he won't try to eat them."

She chuckled at his doubtful expression. "No, he won't. And he's not going to draw your blood, either."

"Right," he said, clearly unconvinced, then leaned close enough that his warm breath teased her ear. "Don't look now. Everyone is watching us."

Showtime. She took the opportunity to lean against his shoulder and run her hand across the wide expanse of his back, just like she'd wanted to do when he took off his shirt at the river. His shiver sent a matching one straight through to her toes.

After a full day's work with Doc Ty, Jessica was glad to be home. This morning, she'd been responsible for one cat, but in only a few hours she'd added two raccoons and was awaiting the arrival of the three police horses and four abandoned miniature goats. She would have quite the menagerie in no time.

Now it was time to introduce Oliver to the raccoons. "Ollie, I'm home," she called out from the front door.

Her big orange cat came around a corner, stretched and sauntered her way. When the kits started chittering, he looked from her to the box and then stood on his hind legs.

"I've brought home some new friends. You have to be extra nice and help me take care of them."

Setting the box on the floor, she pulled back the cardboard flaps and gave Oliver a chance to see the babies. The raccoons huddled in one corner as far away from this new animal as they could get. Once she stroked their little heads and imitated the sound of a mother raccoon, they relaxed a bit. But she stopped Oliver before he jumped in with them. "I don't think they're ready for that much attention from you."

After more sniffing and close inspection, the animals took to one another with no problem. Jessica fed all three animals and then herself before putting together a kennel for the new additions. It had a cozy dark section for sleeping and an open play area with a climbing tree. Once she was showered and chilling on the couch, Jessica did something she'd been putting off. She called Aunt Kay.

Alerting her family that she was seeing someone was one of the ingredients for a successful charade. That way it wouldn't be quite so much of a shock when they eloped.

"Hello, sweetheart. How are you?"

Her aunt's cheery voice made her a touch homesick. "Really good. And I thought you might be interested to know that I'm taking your suggestion to heart. I went on a date with Jake. He's a guy I first met when I came here as a teenager."

"Oh, I'm so glad to hear this." Kay's delight came

through as clearly as if she were in the room. "I can hear it in your voice. You're excited about this guy."

A lot more than I should be. "He's fun to hang out with."

"Tell me everything. Where you went. What he's like. What he does. Is he cute?"

Jessica resisted laughing, knowing firsthand that phone conversations with her aunt could sometimes take a while. "You have to let me talk if you want to hear the answers."

"I'm just so excited for you. But can I put the phone down for a minute and finish making my tea?"

"No problem. I'll wait." Her aunt had yet to get the hang of using speakerphone.

"Then you can tell me everything. Be right back."

Lying back on her overstuffed maroon couch and staring at the beams running across her wooden ceiling, Jessica pictured her aunt moving around the elegant Talbot family home. So different from her log cabin. All day she'd been mentally practicing what to say to Aunt Kay but was worried it was going to come out sounding fake. Maybe if she momentarily pretended her relationship with Jake was real, she could tell a story of how she *imagined* it developing. It should be easier to do since her aunt couldn't see her face and read her expression. She'd act the part of an infatuated woman, then after they hung up, she'd once again go through the list of reasons not to fall for Jake Carter.

She grabbed and notepad off the coffee table and jotted down a few reminders. *Dangerous job. He's moving away, and long-distance relationships never work. He's not looking for a relationship.*

"Okay," Aunt Kay said. "I'm settled in with my tea and ready to hear everything."

"It was a great first date." Jessica told her all about the man who'd given up a job he loved with a K9 unit so he could come home and take care of his dad. The man who jumped into the river with his shoes on to save her, even though she hadn't needed saving.

And as sure as the sun would rise, the one who was trying to steal her heart, no matter how many reasons she wrote down to convince herself otherwise.

Chapter Ten

"I'm home," Jake called out as they stepped inside his front door. "I have someone I want you to meet."

His dad looked up from his book with a huge grin and rose from his favorite leather wingback chair. "This must be your mystery woman?"

Really, Pops?

Jessica's eyebrows arched in a way that told him there would be questions about the whole "mystery woman" thing.

"This is Jessica Talbot. And yes, she is the woman I met on the roadside and didn't know her name. So, for a while, her identity was a mystery."

"Nice to meet you, young lady. I'm Seth Carter but you can call me Pops."

"It's nice to meet you, too. And the truth is, Jake

just didn't remember me. Guess I look a lot different than I did when I was sixteen."

"She's actually in that group photo hanging in the hallway."

"I am?"

"You sure are," Jake said. "I noticed it after the coffee incident but wasn't sure until after the turtle incident."

"Incident?" She propped her hands on her hips and tilted her head. "Is that what we're calling them? Did you write up a report?"

"Maybe." He enjoyed teasing her, especially when her nose scrunched up and her pretty mouth pursed.

"Well, what do you know?" Pops studied her face a moment. "You're the one with the blue hair?"

Jessica's laugh always made Jake smile, even on the inside.

"That's probably me. I need to see this photo." She ran her hand along the dark wood of the archway leading into the living room. "You have a lovely home. It's Craftsman style, right?"

Jake laughed. "You've opened yourself up to a history lesson with that question."

Pops shoved Jake's shoulder good-naturedly.

"I'd love to hear all about it," Jessica said. "And if it's okay, see the rest of the house."

"Absolutely," Pops said. "Come this way."

While his dad gave her the tour and a rundown of the family history, Jake prepped steaks and readied the outdoor grill. With all the baking she'd done for him, the least he could do was feed her a meal.

And he'd needed to introduce her to Pops. Because it was part of the plan, not because he wanted to. It had nothing to do with the feelings Jess stirred.

And maybe if I keep telling myself that, I'll actually talk myself into believing it.

He eventually found them outside on the south side of the house. The pair studied the flower bed as if they were preparing for a very important mission.

"Once I'm healed, maybe next week, I want to plant a variety of ferns and shade plants," Pops said and motioned to a spot under the windows.

Before Jake could say that next week was way too soon for him to do yardwork, Jessica made a sound of obvious disagreement.

"I may not be a human doctor, but I do know that you should not be doing anything so physical as early as next week. It's too soon for you to be digging holes and planting."

Jake wrapped one arm around her shoulders. "You should listen to her. She's a smart lady."

"Fine. But I won't like it," he said with a grin directed at Jessica, then he pointed at Jake. "Guess you get to do the work."

"I'll do it next week." He still had his arm around Jess, and she was rubbing slow circles on his back and making him all gooey inside. He pressed his free hand against his thigh so he wouldn't cradle her against his chest and inhale her honeysuckle scent.

"I can help with the planting," she said.

Jake shook his head. "I don't expect you to do

that. I'm about to put the steaks on the grill. Who's hungry?"

"I am," Pops and Jess said in unison.

Jake and Jessica walked into the house hand in hand, and he wasn't even sure how they'd ended up that way or which one of them had done it.

I'm in a truckload of trouble.

The following day, Jessica worked with Doc Ty all morning, then drove Pops to Green Forest Nursery. She pulled a flatbed cart while Jake's dad picked plants that she would not allow him to lift. On the drive back to his house, they talked casually about this and that and Pops told funny stories about Jake as a kid.

"Has my son told you about his ex-wife?"

Ex-wife? Her stomach clenched along with her hands on the steering wheel. "No. He hasn't mentioned her."

Pops directed one of the AC vents to blow his way. "They married right out of high school."

"He got married when he was eighteen?"

"Nineteen," Pops said. "He didn't take my advice, which was don't do it. But my son is a caretaker and rescues people, and she used that to her advantage."

"That's terrible." Guilt washed over her in a heavy wave.

I'm doing the same thing to him!

But…she was also helping him, she reminded herself. It was mutually beneficial.

"It's a bit of a sore topic, so I guess I'm not surprised he hasn't told you yet. He'll want to kick my butt for telling, but I think it's important for you to know. It might explain why he's a little gun-shy when it comes to relationships. He's a protector, and sometimes he's guards his own heart too much. But I think you're just what he needs, and I hope you'll give him a chance."

"Of course, I will." Some things about Jake were starting to make sense. Why a young, healthy man avoided relationships. His willingness to go to these lengths of planning a fake marriage to help his family. "I won't say anything about our conversation. I'll let Jake be the one to bring it up when he's ready." But that didn't mean she didn't have questions right now. "How long were they married?"

"About a year. He was working for the Oak Hollow police department at the time, but he resigned and left town when the gossip started. Said he wasn't sticking around for a small-town scandal."

She sucked in a breath. "There was a scandal?"

"No, not really, but Jake saw it that way. He was young and hurt and embarrassed, and I can understand that." Pops shook his head. "I could tell the girl was trouble from the day I met her."

"What happened?"

"I knew he wasn't happy but didn't know how bad it had gotten. He tends to keep things to himself. He'd made a commitment and was trying to figure out a way to make it work. The breakup was sudden, and he was blindsided and embarrassed by the things she said around town. Pretty much all lies, and as you can imagine, Jake took it pretty hard."

"What a bit—" She stopped herself before calling his ex a bad name. "That's horrible." She was more familiar than she'd like with the sting of public humiliation caused by a significant other. And she hadn't even been married. She'd only been dating when it happened to her, but it had happened to Jake in a small town, witnessed by everyone he'd grown up with.

"They divorced, and he moved to Dallas where his mom lives. He got a new job with the police force up there."

"What about his ex-wife? Does she still live here?"

"No. She left town before he did. Probably ran off with a circus."

She couldn't help grinning at the expression on his face. Jake occasionally made that same expression with one brow and one side of his mouth arched. They looked a lot alike, but Pops was a bit taller and had gray mixed in with his short brown hair. It was a glimpse that suggested Jake would be a good-looking older man.

"A lot of the townsfolk didn't make her feel very welcome any longer. Not when she started talking about our family. Did you know Jake is the fifth generation of Carters in Oak Hollow?"

"Wow, what history. The house I grew up in hasn't been in our family quite that long. My grandparents built it and my aunt still lives there."

They continued talking about family until all the

plants were unloaded and gathered under a pecan tree. Jessica couldn't yet tell him that she'd soon be a part of the Carter family. But only temporarily.

When Jake got home from work, Jessica's SUV was in front of his house, but she wasn't inside. She was digging a hole in the flower bed and looking way too sexy in another pair of denim shorts and a red tank top, her long hair pulled into a high ponytail. She had earbuds in, and the swaying rhythm of her hips suggested an upbeat song.

There was no way he could ignore the woman visiting his nightly dreams. And he didn't want to.

As he got closer, she caught sight of him, pulled out her earbuds and smiled. "Hi, handsome. How was work?"

She said it in a playful way, but his skin warmed. That was something a wife asked at the end of the day. But…she *would* be his wife. Soon. If only on paper. "My day was good. Uneventful. I see you've been busy. Didn't you have to work today?"

"I was done by noon and took your dad to the nursery. And don't worry, I didn't let him do more than walk and point out what he wanted."

"I didn't think any different. Thanks for looking out for him."

Jessica leaned the shovel against the house. "When I'd hang out at Emma's house during the summers, I remember thinking how quiet it was even in town. After years of not being here, I thought maybe I'd dreamed up that part, but it's true. I can hear birds and the wind and so many natural sounds."

The back screen door opened, then banged closed behind his dad. "Hey, son." Pops handed a glass of ice water to Jessica.

"Thank you." She took a long drink, then pressed the cold glass to her cheek.

Jake couldn't take his eyes from a single drop of sweat gliding slowly down her neck, disappearing between her breasts. "You really didn't have to come and do this work. I would've gotten to it."

She wiggled her dirt-stained fingers. "I don't mind getting my hands dirty. And I like to keep busy."

Pops chuckled. "My ex-wife has a lot of good qualities and is a wonderful woman in many ways, but she wouldn't dream of putting her hands in the dirt. Never wants to break a fingernail. And this one here…" He pointed to Jessica as he spoke to Jake. "She wouldn't let me lift a thing at the nursery. And now she's doing all the work, even though I told her to leave it for you. Your mystery woman is a keeper, son."

Every hair on Jake's arms raised with the kind of goose bumps that could only come from hearing her referred to as his.

But she's not mine to keep.

"You two don't work too hard," Pops said and turned for the back door. "I'm going to follow my doctor's advice and go rest."

Jake looked at Jessica, but she wouldn't meet his gaze. Her pretty smile had slipped away, and he couldn't tell if it was from guilt about fooling people or something else. She picked up the shovel and dug another scoop of dirt.

He hadn't expected to come home and find her hanging out with his dad and working in the yard, and he needed a minute to pull himself together. And remind himself of the plan they'd agreed on. "I'm going to change clothes and then I'll help you finish."

"Okay." Continuing to work with determination, she still didn't glance his way.

A gust of wind cooled the sweat forming on his skin. Was Jess doing this landscaping project because she truly wanted to help his dad, or was it only part of the marriage charade? Just playing a role?

Pops was in the kitchen washing dishes, not resting as he'd said. "I like her. Much better than—" His dad didn't finish the sentence.

"I like her, too, but you don't have to be so obvious with your opinions and matchmaking."

"She knows it's all in good fun. I've only spent a small amount of time with her but enough to know she's a good person."

"I agree. I gotta go change clothes," he said on his way out of the room. He hadn't truly considered how it would feel to trick the people they loved.

Once he'd locked up his service weapon and put on old clothes, he poured a glass of water to take outside. From the kitchen window, he saw the new nosy neighbor—whose name he couldn't remember—making quick strides right for Jessica.

"Oh, no."

Before he could get outside to save Jess from any trouble, he heard the woman's shrill voice.

"Yoo-hoo. Are you doing some landscaping?"

"Yes, I am," Jessica said and wiped dirt from her hands.

Jake held back at the kitchen doorway to see how Jessica would handle their nosy neighbor.

"Who are you? I don't know you."

"I'm Jessica Talbot, and I'm new in town."

"Do the Carters know you are doing this?"

Jess stifled a laugh with a cough behind her fist. "Yes. I don't make a habit of going around working in people's yards without them knowing about it."

The woman's pinched-face attempt at smiling was priceless.

"What kind of plants are you putting over there?" the neighbor asked.

"Looks like ferns and caladiums," Jake said and motioned to the cluster of potted plants literally right beside the neighbor's feet.

Jessica stepped out of the flower bed to stand beside Jake and grinned at his eye roll.

The middle-aged woman bent for a closer inspection. "They don't have flowers?" She tapped her finger on her chin. "And you got this approved by the architectural control committee? You know there are rules to keep our neighborhood looking good."

Jess turned her back to hide barely restrained laughter.

"We're well aware of the rules," he said. "My

family has lived here a lot longer than you. Have a good evening." He took Jessica's hand and led her toward the kitchen door, leaving Mrs. Nosy to sputter to herself.

"She's a Gladys Kravitz," Jessica said under her breath.

It took Jake a second to catch what she meant by that, then he chuckled and squeezed her hand. "Now I truly understand the meaning of that nickname."

In such a short time, he and Jessica already shared inside jokes. Her fun-loving attitude always lightened his mood, and he wanted to believe that her being here was not just to get on anyone's good side or to play the role of his fake girlfriend. But he couldn't risk letting his guard down too much. He'd be leaving Oak Hollow for a job that was very important to him. Enjoying her company for now was one thing, but opening his heart was another.

She went straight to the kitchen sink and turned on the water.

"We'll wait until she goes home, then finish the planting," he said.

"Are all of your neighbors this...involved?"

"No. Our neighbor on the other side of our house is wonderful. She used to feed my dog, and she waters the plants and that kind of stuff. The only one to watch out for is Gladys Kravitz."

"Gladys Kravitz?" Pops asked as he came into the kitchen.

Jake locked eyes with Jessica, and they shared a smile. "The new neighbor on that side of our house."

"Oh, her," Pops said and got out sandwich makings. "She just needs a little time to relax and get used to small-town life."

Jessica took a seat at the kitchen table. "You're probably right. Just laugh it off for now."

"You'll like most of our neighbors once you get to know them," Pops promised.

Jake felt slightly dizzy. His dad's statement made it sound as if she'd become a part of the family and would be around for holidays and Sunday dinners. Like their relationship was real.

Pops opened a loaf of bread. "Tell me about the vet practice you plan to open."

Her eyes lit up. "It's going to be on my ranch along with a wildlife rescue. At some point I'll need to hire a few employees, and of course I'll make house calls to see large farm animals when needed."

The excitement in Jessica's voice matched her smile. Jake's gut told him Jessica Talbot was truly a good person who went out of her way to help others. It was no act.

She deserves to have someone help her, too.

As difficult as their fake relationship would be, he'd do it for her.

Chapter Eleven

Jake pulled up to Jessica's log cabin the next evening, as ready as he'd ever be for public date number two. Time to draw on his poor acting skills and perform. But in truth, he'd discovered that playing the part of an infatuated guy wasn't as difficult as he'd thought it would be. The struggle was keeping his eyes and hands off Jess when they were alone.

Before he could get to her door, she breezed down the front steps, and his pulse instantly revved up a notch. In an off-the-shoulder black top and jeans, she looked gorgeous, but it wasn't just what she wore that caught his eye, it was the mystery woman herself. Always surprising him. He met her at the passenger side and opened the door.

"Can I catch a ride to town, Officer?"

She made him feel playful in a way he hadn't allowed himself in a long time. "Evenin', ma'am, only if you'll let me take you dancin'?" he asked with an exaggerated Southern accent that allowed him to hear the music of her laughter.

"I'd love to."

Do not kiss her. Don't even touch her.

After closing her door, he went to his side and got in.

"So, tell me more about where we're going and the band playing."

"It's got indoor and outdoor stages and dance floors, and a playground for families with kids. The band is called the Nature Boys. Alexandra will probably be there and sing a few songs because it's her dad's band."

"Cool. Music therapist, artist and singer. Alexandra sure has a lot of talents."

"I could say the same for you. Changing flat tires, baking and rescuing turtles and raccoons."

"You forgot gardening."

He couldn't wait to discover what other talents she possessed.

The band had already started the first set when they found seats at a table near the outdoor dance floor. Couples twirled past and a group of little children ran by on their way to the playground.

"Do you want kids someday?" she asked.

The question made something shift in his chest. He'd thought he'd have one or two by now. "Sure. But

I'm glad I didn't have any with—" He hadn't told her he'd been married. "I have an ex-wife."

She nodded and looked down at her hands. "How long were you married?"

"Barely over a year. Want something to drink?"

"Yes, please. Surprise me."

He should probably tell her more about his sham of a marriage, and he would, but he didn't have to do it right now.

When he neared their table with drinks, Jessica was standing at the railing around the dance floor, and there was already another guy he didn't know standing beside her. He was supposed to *pretend* to be jealous. Not feel it for real. Jake moved close enough to overhear the other man.

"I saw you watching everyone and thought you might like to dance?"

When she returned the guy's smile, Jake gritted his teeth and wanted to intervene, but he had no right to step in. *Do I?*

"It's so nice of you to ask," Jessica said. "But I'm here with someone."

Good answer, Mystery Woman.

Holding the necks of the beer bottles with one hand, he slid his free arm around her waist and nodded to the other man in greeting. "Evening."

Props to the guy for tipping his hat and wishing them a good night.

Jessica took a beer and grinned. "You're a better actor than you let on. You had him backing away in a hurry."

He shrugged, downing a healthy swallow of beer. "I didn't do anything. You're the one who turned him down." Had she picked up on his jealousy? "Do you know how to dance?"

"I know how to waltz because my grandfather taught me when I was a kid, but this is different, and not every couple is doing it exactly the same. Will you teach me?" She leaned in close to whisper. "It will get eyes on us and tongues talking."

Did she really have to mention tongues when he was already fighting the urge to kiss her? And everyone's eyes were already on them. "Let's give them something to talk about."

And an excuse for me to hold you.

Her smile made his belly flip. This might be more physical contact than he could safely handle, but it was too late for a U-turn. Jake led her onto the dance floor and, satisfied with their position on the edge, he wrapped his free arm around her waist. With a bit more enthusiasm than he'd planned, he brought their bodies close. Hip to hip, their inhales catching in unison.

Her brown eyes dilated, and Jessica slid her hand around the back of his neck, her deep inhale causing her chest to rise against his. He only had to tilt his head down slightly to meet her eyes and see her soft skin shimmer in the lights.

The song was slow and the perfect beat to teach her to two-step. Instead of giving her step-by-step instructions like take two steps with that foot and one with the other, he couldn't resist testing a theory.

"I'm not going to tell you what steps to take. Follow my movements. Feel the beat and move with me."

"Okay." Her voice was barely a whisper.

He'd always hoped there was a partner meant for him. One who fit. One who complemented him.

He swept her into the dance. Their first few steps were clumsy, but a few bars into the song their rhythms synced. She followed every move, even when he spun them around. He didn't usually hold a woman this close while dancing, especially after only knowing her such a short time, but it was easier to teach her with their bodies touching.

At least that's what he told himself, right before tipping his head to rest his cheek against the side of her forehead.

If you'd asked her yesterday, Jessica would've said she did not like country music. But tonight, she loved it. Maybe it was the beat or the deep smooth cadence of the singer's voice. Maybe it was the man holding her in his arms, enticing her body to move in perfect harmony with his.

I could dance like this all night long.

When she raised her head and their cheeks brushed, his was smooth from a fresh shave, and his fingers flexed low on her back. A delicious spark shot along her spine, and her senses awoke from a deep sleep.

He's making me feel...everything.

The brush of his thigh against hers. The beat of their hearts. The rise and fall of her breast against his muscled chest. And with the slightest shift of her head, the corner of her lips against his. It was as close as you could get to a kiss without actually kissing. With her eyes closed, she let him take her into a magical moment where it was only the two of them. Their surroundings faded and the fact that they were supposed to be acting was forgotten. They moved straight into song after song.

Finally the band announced a short break, and she wanted to beg them to keep playing.

Jessica didn't want to let go of him or this new sparkly feeling. Didn't want to meet his eyes and not see her feelings reflected in his gaze. Hand in hand, and without a word or glance, they walked off the dance floor. Maybe their relationship wouldn't have to be as fake as they'd thought? He *was* still holding her hand in a way that felt like more than pretend. She'd never tried the friends with benefits thing, but it was suddenly tempting.

Back at their table, their seats had been taken, so they stood at the railing. Jake lightly squeezed her fingers before letting go. "You're a good dancer. And that was a very convincing performance."

Her stomach clenched, and she opened her mouth to admit she wasn't pretending but swallowed back the statement. "Thanks. You, too."

"We're not so bad at this, after all."

She didn't mention that it would be difficult for her to fake attraction like this. Impossible, really. But what about him? Was he just a better actor than he'd let on? "I guess my rules for…relationships help guide me."

"What are your rules?"

"Number one is never fall for a guy with a dangerous job." He was standing close enough that she felt him flinch. Saying that to a police officer was probably in poor taste, but he needed to know where she was coming from.

"Why is that number one?"

"My father was a bodyguard and was killed in the line of duty."

"I'm sorry," he said and gave her a quick side hug. "That must have been really hard."

"Yes, it was." The back of her throat tightened as she held back tears. "I don't ever want to repeat that kind of pain or have to worry about someone every single day."

"I get that. There's Luke and Alexandra over on the other side of the dance floor. And walking up to them now are Jenny and Eric, the couple getting married next weekend. They said I could bring a plus one. If I take you to the wedding, everyone will know we're…"

"Dating?" Jessica finished for him and hooked her arm through his. "Let's go over there so I can meet them."

"Didn't you meet Jenny at book club?"

"No. She wasn't able to make it because she was working on her wedding dress. They are gorgeous."

He rolled his eyes and maneuvered them through the crowd. "Every woman says that about Eric."

She giggled. "I was talking about them together. As a couple. But now that you mention it, he is rather easy on the eyes. They will make beautiful babies together."

"He already has a little girl. But they'll probably have more."

Introductions were made and another round of drinks ordered. The groom-to-be looked uncomfortable in the crowd. He was tall and broad with shoulder-length hair and resembled a brooding Highland warrior, but when he smiled, it revealed his heart and love for Jenny.

Jenny was every bit the glowing bride-to-be. Her dark waist-length hair glistened in the stage lights, and she excitedly shared details of their upcoming outdoor wedding. She made Jessica promise she'd be there with Jake. Being with the other couples kept Jessica from obsessing and overanalyzing the sizzling chemistry she'd shared with Jake on the dance floor.

They danced a few more times, but Jake kept distance between them. And this time it did feel more like an act.

When they drove up to Jessica's house at the end of the evening, Jake left his truck running and stared out the front windshield. She studied his handsome profile. The tension creasing his forehead. His jaw tensing as he clenched his teeth. His two-handed grip on the steering wheel. A clear message that the night was over, and it was time to get out of his truck.

An empty sensation grabbed the pit of her stomach. "I think date number two was a success. Do you not agree?"

"I agree." He glanced her way, very briefly. "I think everyone is talking about us."

Oh, maybe that's the problem. He doesn't like being the topic of gossip. "Thanks for teaching me how to dance to country music."

"You're welcome."

"What time does the Acorn Festival start tomorrow?"

"Ten. Should I pick you up in the morning?"

He finally met her eyes, but she did not read enthusiasm in his baby blues. Maybe picking her up was too much like *real* dating. And they were just friends playing a role. "No need," she said. "I'll drive into town and meet you at your house, then we can walk over to the square together. It'll save you a trip out here."

"That works." He nodded once but continued to stare out the windshield with both hands on the steering wheel.

An ache took up residence in her chest. Such a difference from how she felt when he was holding her on the dance floor not so long ago. "I'll see you in the morning."

"Sounds good." He held out his fist as if waiting for the kind of knuckle bump men exchange.

Unsure what else to do, she bumped her fist against his, then fumbled for the door handle in her rush to get out. "Good night," she said over her shoulder.

Their connection on the dance floor suddenly seemed like a dream.

He waited until she had her door unlocked before driving away, his red taillights bobbing over bumps in her gravel driveway. Oliver trotted over to greet her, then propped both front paws on her leg.

"Hello, good boy." Jessica lifted him into her arms, then got comfy on the couch. She could hear the raccoons chittering in their kennel in the kitchen. "Are you going to help me feed the kits?" With an insistent meow that turned to purring, Oliver rubbed his head on her chin.

"Well, since you're asking, let me tell you the condensed version of tonight's performance. Jake swept me off my feet on the dance floor, then said good night like I'm one of his buddies. I think I've been reminded of my place in the friend zone."

Had she imagined the sexual tension on the dance floor? Had it only been her having a chemical reaction to his touch? Their marriage charade's biggest challenge was not going to be their fake dates or even convincing people their marriage was real. For her, it would be playing the part of a good buddy when they were alone.

Chapter Twelve

"Did I really tell her good night with a fist bump?" Jake asked himself for the fifth time since waking up at daybreak. He poured another cup of coffee and looked out at the birds gathered at his neighbor's feeder.

I'm such a bonehead. Why didn't I just tell her good night or say see you tomorrow?

Anything would've been better than his awkward attempt to… Whatever it was he was trying to do.

I'm trying to protect my heart.

What had started as a fun evening had turned molten on the dance floor, but Jessica's rule against dating a guy with a dangerous job had hit him like a sucker punch. His ex-wife's face had flashed before his eyes in a painful rush. He absolutely could not fall for Jessica only to have her leave him because of his job. A job he loved.

So, in the middle of their second date, he'd slammed on the brakes before his heart even thought about following his desires. His libido was more awake than it had been in years. Maybe ever. This whole…what had she called it?

Charade.

Whatever name you gave it, their time together would be a test of his resistance and frustration tolerance level. He'd made promises and keeping them was important. Jess was counting on him. He could not fall in love, but there was no guarantee he'd resist something physical if she wanted to take things there.

By the time Jessica arrived at his house, he had talked himself down from alarm to determination. He'd play this role, help them both and not let any deep emotions get involved.

"Good morning," he said and returned her wave from his front porch. As she rounded the hood of her SUV, his jaw clenched. Her blue skirt hit midthigh and showed off legs that were sure to draw every guy's attention. It wasn't too short, but short enough to tempt.

"Sorry I'm late," she said. "I had to feed the raccoons and they were more interested in playing."

"No problem. You're not late." He crossed the porch and met her at the front door. "Do you want to come inside or head over to the square?"

"I'm ready to go, if you are."

They walked along his shady street, and he reminded himself that they could have fun together, like the day at the river. But then he remembered that moment when they'd come so close to kissing in the water. She'd been all wet and glistening, and he'd wanted to suck the water off the curve of her neck. And then on the dance floor...

I need to stop thinking about that.

"It's going to be hot today." Jessica pulled her long hair into a ponytail and secured it with an elastic band from her wrist.

"It is." She had no idea just how hot she was making him. Much more and he might combust and take her with him into their own little world of pleasure.

"Can you stop by after work tomorrow and help me get the pen ready for the miniature goats?"

"Sure. I can do that."

She gasped when the toe of her flip-flop caught on a spot in the sidewalk where a tree root had cracked and raised the concrete.

He caught her arm before she could fall. "I've got you."

"Thanks for the save, Officer." Rather than letting go, she looped her arm around his.

Every time she touched him, he had a little more trouble resisting. "Happy to assist. At least you didn't take me down with you this time." It still surprised him when she laughed rather than taking offense.

"Thank goodness." She glanced around at the other people filing toward the square and the Acorn Festival. "It's so much worse when a lot of people are around to witness my clumsiness. Embarrassing myself is one thing, but I'd hate to include you in the incident."

"If I can handle the turtle incident, falling down would be nothing." He kissed her cheek before he realized what he was doing, his lips tingling from the contact, and he received a bright smile in return.

Their easy flowing conversation had him relaxed by the time they joined the crowd of people. Until... he noticed other men noticing her. As predicted, her beauty drew many eyes her way. His protective instinct was so amped up he gave one cowboy the stare and had the urge to growl at another. At this rate, he'd need a beer before lunchtime.

What is wrong with me? It wasn't like him to be this...jealous.

Jessica hadn't been able to stop thinking about the awkward way they had parted last night, and it had led to her dreaming about Jake ending their agreement. Being nervous about their secret plan was expected, but they'd had moments of easy playfulness and she trusted they could get back to that. If his kiss on her cheek was any indication, today's public outing would help them relax and remember they could have fun together.

The town square had been transformed into a colorful party. It was closed to traffic and filled with booths of food capable of blowing anyone's diet, handmade art and entertainment on two stages. Alexandra and her father were on the small stage, just their guitars and beautifully harmonizing voices.

When Jessica spotted the pet adoption in front of the courthouse, she took Jake's hand and tugged him in that direction. "Let's go see if they have any dogs that are good candidates for you. What breeds or qualities are you looking for?"

"Ideally, a German shepherd." He waved to a passing family. "And I want a young dog so there aren't many bad habits in place."

As they walked hand in hand across the center of the square, he didn't tense or shy away from her touch. But they *were* here to be seen acting like a couple. She could not read more into this than Jake just being a better actor than he'd claimed. "Tell me how you became interested in working with dogs?"

"Pops and I took one to obedience training when I was a kid and that got me hooked on the idea. I was in high school when my interest moved into training rescue and service dogs. I started my career with the Oak Hollow police department, but after my divorce I ended up in Dallas where they have a K9 unit."

She enjoyed listening to him talk. His smooth deep voice rolled easily over her ears. "And you picked Dallas because your mom lives there?"

"Yes. She had already moved there years before, and she has a friend on the force who talked me into coming." He sighed and glanced around. "At first, I had to live with my mom. But only until I got a couple of paychecks and found an apartment."

"Living with her wasn't a good fit?"

"Not ideal. I'll tell you more about her in a minute. While I was working with the K9 unit, I got all my training certifications." He kneeled beside a large pen holding a litter of adorable puppies. A fluffy black-and-white one trotted over to sniff his hand.

"Oh, he's a cutie," Jessica said.

Just as Jake picked up the animal, a little boy gasped. He had the most crestfallen expression and was holding the hand of a beautiful dark-haired woman who had her eyes set on the man, not the puppy.

"It's okay, honey." The woman patted her child's back but kept smiling at Jake. "There are lots of other dogs."

Jake held out the pup. "Is this the one you like?"

"Yes, sir." The child's lip quivered.

"I can tell he likes you, too. I'm not taking him."

The kid looked from Jake to his mom, and at her nod, he smiled and accepted the wiggling ball of fluff. "Thank you, Officer Carter."

"You're welcome, kiddo."

The mom fluttered her long, thick eyelashes at Jake. "Maybe Officer Carter will help us train this puppy?"

Jessica would swear the other woman shot her an expression that warned of competition.

Jake stood and dusted grass from the knees of his jeans. "I have a good puppy training book I can recommend."

Now, it was the mother who wore the crestfallen expression, and Jessica had to hide her grin. Once they walked away to adopt the little boy's new puppy, she bumped her shoulder against Jake's. "That was very sweet of you. And I'm pretty sure his mom is sweet on *you*."

He made a grumbly sound in his throat. "Why do you think I offered the book and not my personal services?"

"I think personal service is what she's hoping for." Jessica laughed at his sour expression. "She's not your type?"

"She is the type who leaves wedding magazines on my desk after three dates."

Jessica gasped. "She did that?"

"No. But another woman did. Three dates and she started hinting at a trip down the aisle with strategically placed bridal magazines."

With a whoosh, her heart seemed to skip a beat. "Um, I think I have her beat." Jessica tipped her head closer to his ear. "I went *all* the way straight out of the gate." His shiver vibrated against her arm. Was it from her statement or her breath against his skin?

"But she wanted a *real* marriage," he said.

His lips were inches from her cheek and, this time, she was the one shivering at the puff of warm breath against her skin. But his words hit like a punch to the gut. He was not giving her "real." She was getting the pretend version of what it would be like to date Jake Carter. Only a look at what she could have but not a taste. Like looking into a bakery window filled with world-famous cupcakes and never being able to go inside.

They were silent for a moment, but when he walked in a wide arc around the cats—as if they'd stretch out their claws and swat him—she couldn't help chuckling. "You don't think I should get a friend for Oliver?"

He shook his head, and with an arm around her waist, he playfully guided her away from the felines. "He already has two raccoons to play with."

His smile gave her that glittery feeling, and she decided to focus on enjoying the day.

They walked among the pens and crates, stopping now and then to look more closely at an animal. But none of the dogs were right for Jake. Once they'd seen all the adorable animals, Jessica promised the fire chief she'd help out with the event next year and met several prospective clients while they adopted pets.

"So, back to the topic of my mom," he said. "Did I tell you she will be here today?"

Her heart gave a little leap. "No. You did not." She hadn't prepared to meet another parent. "Should I be worried?"

"No."

"The expression on your face says differently." She brushed one finger over the creases between his eyes.

He sighed. "Let's just say, Jewels Carter is not shy about asking personal questions or giving advice and opinions whether someone wants them or not. She has a way of getting to the bottom of things. We tease her that she should've been a police interrogator."

"Dude, are you kidding me?" She came to a complete stop beside a snow cone booth. "A little more warning would've been nice. I thought you said I shouldn't be worried?"

"You'll be fine. Look how you hit it off with Pops. You've done great with him."

"I'll do my best." She dropped her voice to a whisper. "Got any tips for withstanding her interrogation? Because our arrangement must stay a secret."

"It will. With my mom, it's best to just let a lot of what she says roll off your back. I have faith you won't let the cat out of the cage."

His expression made her smile. "We're doing so much whispering, people will be thinking we have tons of secrets."

"We have a few."

The delicious scent of caramelized sugar drifted on the warm breeze. "Oh, I smell caramel corn. I definitely need some."

As they waited in the crowded food line, he stood close enough that she could feel the heat of his body on her back. The woman and little boy from the pet adoption were in the line next to them, and the mother was once again gazing at Jake. Jessica took the opportunity to lean against him. His hands went to her hips, and she tipped her head to grin at him. "Your fans are watching."

He nuzzled his cheek against hers and sent sparkles dancing across her skin, but she couldn't be sure if it was to send a message to the woman or because he just wanted to. Before she had time to think too much about it, the girl behind the counter took their order.

They walked and ate mostly in silence, checking out what vendors had to offer. There was everything from woodcarving, pottery, paintings and jewelry to a booth selling baby oak trees.

"What did Pops say when you quit your job in Dallas and came home?"

"He was mad that I'd left a job I loved, but I told him I wanted to try one more time to talk Oak Hollow into adding a K9 unit. Which was true."

"But they still won't consider it?"

"Nope. They said it's not the right time."

"But maybe someday?"

He shrugged. "Maybe."

Foolish or not, there was a part of her that hoped he might stay or at least come back to Oak Hollow one day. Jessica sensed a subtle change in his demeanor and followed his gaze. "What's wrong?"

"There's my mom. The one carrying the big straw bag with flowers on it."

The woman was overdressed for an outdoor festival but very well put together. Blond hair in a sleek, perfect bun at the nape of her neck. A crisp white button-up with three-quarter-length sleeves, red capris and kitten-heel sandals.

"Ready to meet her?"

"Now is as good of a time as any." When he laced his fingers with hers, she couldn't help but take strength from his touch. They made their way through the crowd to where his mom rushed for an empty picnic table in the shade of an oak tree.

She caught sight of them and waved like a queen on a parade float. "Son, there you are. I've been looking for you."

"Here I am. Jess, this is my mother, Jewels Carter. Mom, this is Dr. Jessica Talbot. My girlfriend."

"A doctor. How impressive." His mom glanced not so subtly at their joined hands. "And I am so glad you are dating again. What is your specialty?"

"Animals," Jessica said and watched his mother's big smile fizzle into a confused sort of expression. "I'm a veterinarian."

"Oh, that's great."

Jessica wasn't sure whether to be offended or amused and was glad she'd been warned about what to expect. Jake let go of her hand to wrap his arm around her waist, and she was grateful for the support.

"She's a really good vet and has a lot to be proud of," Jake said.

"Of course. Wonderful accomplishment." Jewels put a hand on her son's arm. "Could you please go get glasses of lemonade for all of us? Jessica and I will sit here at this picnic table in the shade and chat while you do."

A glimmer of panic swirled through Jessica. Was she about to get the third degree to see if she met with his mother's approval?

Jake tightened his hold around her waist, and she gave him her best *I can do this* expression. The fact that he was checking with her before just walking away was a comfort.

"I would love some lemonade." Jessica returned his smile before he walked toward a booth topped with a giant lemon.

I've been in more difficult situations. I can do this. No problem.

Now that her pep talk was finished, she would not let any of his mom's questions trip her up. Sitting face-to-face with her across a picnic table, Jessica noticed the precision of her makeup application, lipstick and all. Jewels was beautiful and looked too young to have a thirty-two-year-old child. She'd passed along her blue eyes to her son. And even though some of her words were a bit sharp, her eyes held care and kindness.

"How long will you be in town?" Jessica asked.

"I have to leave tomorrow. This was a quick trip, but I couldn't miss the Acorn Festival. Have you bought a house? I know a great Realtor in town."

"I already bought a place. The ranch that belonged to the Williams family."

"The whole ranch? And you live out there in the country all by yourself?"

"For now."

"I guess since you've bought that much property, you plan to settle permanently in Oak Hollow?"

"Yes. I'm opening a veterinary practice."

Jewels cleared her throat and glanced at her son standing in line. "I don't know if Jake has told you, but he's moving back to Dallas. He has the opportunity to advance his career there."

"He told me. You must be so proud of him."

"I am." She pulled a folding fan from her bag and spread it open to reveal a floral design on red silk. "I don't want to see him pass up advancement."

"I can understand that." The message was clear. His mother was warning her not to get in the way of his career. How mad would she be when they eloped? Jessica tried to swallow the prickly lump in her throat. Jewels was looking out for her son, and she understood. Her father would've done the same.

"Here you go, ladies," Jake said.

Jessica took the glass of lemonade. "Thank you. I was just telling your mother about my ranch."

He gave his mom her glass and sat beside Jessica. "It's a beautiful place. Good fishing."

Sipping her drink and fanning herself, Jewels studied both of them. "But out in the country all by yourself? You're not scared?"

"No. I was more frightened in the city."

"The city is where Jake has more opportunity for promotions and good pay. I'll be happy to have him living close to me again. And his furniture out of my garage."

"Mom, I'm sitting right here. You don't have to talk about me like I'm not."

Jewels waved her fan in his direction. "I'm just a proud mom."

His mother was not the most subtle of women. Pops was a joy to be around, but Jewels might take a bit more effort.

What am I getting myself into?

Chapter Thirteen

After a day at the Acorn Festival and a thorough interrogation from Jewels Carter, Jake followed Jessica to her ranch for a home-cooked dinner. And probably to see if his mom had scared her off. As she cooked, Jake sat on the living room floor playing with the baby raccoons. One had climbed his shirt and was curled up in the crook of his arm. The other was trying to crawl up his pant leg. Oliver was outside because he wouldn't have stood for the rascals she'd named Loki and Floki getting cuddles while he did not, and Jake wasn't ready for this kind of attention from a feline.

With music playing softly in the background and the aroma of garlic bread and pasta sauce wafting through the air, it was a very domestic, although somewhat unusual scene.

"You'll let Loki and Floki climb all over you, but not my sweet cat?"

"I'm working on it." He put the kits back into their kennel and washed his hands. "I gave Oliver's head a scratch when he came over to sniff me."

Jessica turned from the stovetop and held out a spoonful of sauce. "Tell me if it needs more salt."

"Mmm. That's really good just like it is."

"It needs a few more minutes to simmer." She turned away before she followed through on her desire to kiss him. After one more stir, she set aside the spoon and turned in time to catch him watching her.

Leaning back against the island, Jake crossed his arms over his broad chest, displaying his muscles in a very nice way. Her body grew warm, and it was not because she was standing beside the stove. Would she ever get the chance to explore all those muscles? Skin to skin?

"Pops talks about you all the time. You're a major hit with him, and he doesn't suspect a thing about our charade."

While she'd been at Jake's house with Pops, nothing about it had felt pretend. "I can't help but notice you didn't say I was a hit with your mother."

"Actually, you were. She's a tougher one to win over, but you did great."

"I haven't spent enough time with her to get a good feel for how we'll get along. But your dad made me feel comfortable right away. I genuinely like Pops. I would've helped him even if he wasn't your dad."

"I believe that. He's going to be happy when we come home married one of these days." Jake glanced at his boots with a frown. "My mom might not be as excited, but it'll all work out in the end."

But will it?

Tension grabbed hold of her body. "Are you feeling bad about fooling everyone? Because I kind of am."

"Yeah. Me, too. But I think our career goals will be enough to explain our mutual breakup. Added to jumping into things too fast." He rubbed his eyes. "I've done it before, so most people won't be surprised."

"Done what?" She had a feeling he was about to tell her more about his ex-wife.

"Got married and divorced quickly. But honestly, a legal piece of paper won't change our relationship from what it is right now. We'll just continue as we are."

Jessica made a noise that she hoped conveyed agreement and quickly turned to pull the garlic bread from the oven. After witnessing her aunt suffer through two unhappy marriages, she'd convinced herself marriage wasn't for her, but after spending time with Jake and her new friends, her heart was making her think twice about the value of such a union.

But I can't forget the danger of his job.

He'd probably be able to play this whole thing out, end it and then move on with his life in Dallas.

But for her… This brilliantly stupid scheme was destined to leave her healing a broken heart and ducking her head in embarrassment, regardless of how they played off their breakup.

"Can we get the marriage license in San Antonio the same day as the wedding?" she asked.

"No. In Texas there is a seventy-two-hour waiting period before you can get married. Guess it gives a person a chance to cut and run."

She arched an eyebrow. "Is that right?"

"We definitely can't get it from the clerk at the Oak Hollow courthouse. Not unless we want everyone to know. Someone might…" He scratched his chin. "Someone will say it's too soon and try to talk us out of it."

Her stomach dropped, and she met his eyes. "Jake, what are we doing?"

He closed the distance between them, and it took a moment before he answered. "What we have to."

"What if this whole thing blows up on us? What if we mess everything up? I don't want people to know the truth of our agreement. Not ever. I don't want to be known as the woman who couldn't get a guy the regular way and had to resort to bribery to get a husband."

Jake's eyebrows shot toward his hairline and his mouth formed a hard line. "And you think *I* want to be known as the guy who got paid to get married? The guy who took money from his rich pretend wife?"

Pretend wife?

Her ex's cutting words bubbled to the surface. *"You're the kind of woman a man dates. You don't have the qualities to be a wife or have a long-term relationship."* He'd made her feel like a placeholder until something better came along. Her throat clogged with emotion, and she turned away so Jake wouldn't see the tears gathering in her eyes. Would anyone ever choose her simply for her? Not her name. Not her connections.

And not her money.

Jake didn't love her. He hadn't chosen her. She'd had to bribe him into marriage. A temporary one that would end. And when it ended… She'd be a divorced woman. A wave of dizziness swept through her, and she braced her forearms on the cool countertop.

"Hey, what's wrong?" Jake put his hands on her shoulders and gently massaged her tense muscles.

After a deep breath, she turned to face him. "Nothing. I'm fine."

His brow creased. "You are not. You're pale as snow." He scooped her into his arms.

She gasped and wrapped her arms around his neck. "What are you doing?" No man had ever carried her like this, cradled against his chest.

"Taking you to the…" He changed direction away from her bedroom. "To the couch before you pass out on the kitchen floor."

She didn't argue because she couldn't find the

right words or the willpower to let go of him. For multiple reasons, she needed this comfort more than she had realized. Plus, she was afraid she'd cry if she opened her mouth. Being held in his arms stirred up the feelings she kept trying to deny. Ones that needed to be kept under lock and key. But this proved there was at least some emotional connection between them. He cared about her well-being.

But he doesn't love me.

Was opening her own veterinary practice worth this charade? Worth the embarrassment if their marriage of convenience was discovered?

Jake leaned forward to put her on the couch, but with her still clinging to him like Velcro, he turned around and sat with her on his lap.

And that caring gesture did it. Big silent tears streamed down her cheeks, and she rested her head on his shoulder.

He wrapped his arms around her a little tighter. "What's wrong, Mystery Woman? Talk to me."

The nickname he'd used once before made her lift her head from his shoulder and look at him while wiping her cheeks. "Sorry. I just let old memories bubble up."

"Want to tell me?"

She suddenly became very aware of being on his lap. The spicy scent of shaving cream. His hand rubbing her back. And she couldn't think while being held in his arms. Reluctantly, she moved from his lap to the cushion beside him. "I've mentioned my last boyfriend, who didn't leave me feeling good about myself."

"Do I need to hunt him down for a man-to-man conversation?"

That made her smile. "No, thanks."

"What did he do?"

"Our relationship started out in an ordinary way. Well, at least I thought it did. I discovered later that he only asked me out because of who my dad was. When I confronted him about it, he admitted to asking me out in hopes of getting a job with my father's company. Said it was a perk that I was pretty, but after the first date it had turned into the real thing for him. But it was a lie."

"Did you break up with him?"

"I'm embarrassed to admit I did not. But I really, really wish that I had. It was a party at his house, and all the guests were there, but he wasn't home yet. His friends and some of mine were in the backyard while I prepped food. He called, and because my hands were wet, I used one finger and hit speakerphone right as a group of people walked into the kitchen."

"Oh, man. I think I see where this might be going." His gaze was fixed on her with interest.

The ocean-blue of his eyes made her momentarily forget what she was talking about.

"And then?" he asked. "Did your guests overhear something private?"

Get it together, Jess.

"So, I'm talking hands free while the guests remain respectfully quiet. I asked when he'd be home and was confused when he said I should come out to the driveway. I thought he just wanted me to help carry in the liquor and food and told him I was cooking and would send someone else to help. So…they all heard the bombshell." Jessica tucked her legs under her and rubbed her arms. "He said it would be a good idea for me to go home. I just kind of froze in place, trying to figure out what caused this request, so I wasn't really thinking about the other people in the room. But I should've been. I knew something bad was coming."

"No one said anything like 'Hey, dude, you're on speakerphone'?"

"No, unfortunately not. Before I could end the call, he said, and this is almost word for word, 'I have brought someone home with me. A woman. I don't want to embarrass you by just walking in with her and want to give you a chance to quietly slip out.'"

"No. Freaking. Way," Jake said, his expression both shocked and angry. "What were your friends doing?"

"Standing there with varying expressions of surprise and sympathy. And then…he said the worst part. 'Jessica, we've had some fun, but I've found someone who is the kind of woman you marry.'"

"What an asshole," Jake growled.

"That's when someone's wife reached over and ended the call. I dipped my fingers into the cocktail sauce and wiped my hands on one of his favorite white linen hand towels, grabbed my purse and left."

"Wait. He had a favorite hand towel?" His lip curled like he'd just smelled something disgusting.

"Yep."

"Did you have to walk past him and this woman on your way out?"

"Oh, yes. At least she had the manners to look uncomfortable and embarrassed. But him… He walked my way, saying something about what he needed in his life, and that's when I told him the 1950s called and wanted their attitude back. And of course, that couldn't be the end of the embarrassment. Several people told several others and soon everyone was talking about it. Within minutes, it became the newest topic of gossip." She let out a long breath and rested her head on the back of the couch. "I was mortified."

"That sucks. Big-time. I'd never do something like that." He rubbed a slow path up and down her arm.

"That experience is the second reason why I am so concerned about anyone discovering our secret. Not only would I not get access to my money, but I can't deal with another public humiliation."

"For the record…" He brushed her hair back from her cheek. "You are the marrying kind. No doubt in my mind. But if you don't want to go through with this, I'll understand."

"But your house. I know how much it means to you and Pops. The way he toured me around proudly telling me your family history made it obvious. And now that I've worked in the yard and dealt with Gladys Kravitz, I feel like I have a stake in it, too."

They shared a quick smile. "I'm good with going ahead with our plan, if you are?"

"Let's agree that neither of us will ever tell anyone our secret. Not family or friends. And not even after it's over."

"Agreed." She took a deep breath. "But when we break up, I guess we can't avoid some level of embarrassment."

He snapped his fingers. "I have an idea... What if when I move to Dallas, we say we're going to stay married and live apart with plans to see one another frequently? Dallas is only six hours away. Then over time we can just let everyone believe we've drifted apart."

"That's a good idea. We could kind of ease into the breakup. I know firsthand that long distance relationships don't work. I tried it for a few years in college."

"I've never been in a long-distance relationship," he said. "At the festival today, several people asked me about my new girlfriend, so I think everyone considers us an official couple."

"Guess we've fooled everyone."

I just need to be honest and not fool myself.

Chapter Fourteen

On a surprisingly cool evening—which meant seventy-five degrees instead of ninety something—Jake drove out to the ranch to pick up Jessica for Jenny and Eric's wedding. They had come to a point in their relationship where she'd said that since he'd soon be living there, they might as well get used to him coming and going. He still knocked before stepping inside. "Jess, I'm here."

"I'll be out in a minute," she called from the bedroom.

Heading for the kitchen, he came face-to-face with his cat adversary. "Look, dude. We're going to have to come to an understanding before I move in. Some amount of distance is good. Sitting near me is one thing, but you will not be sitting on my lap or sleeping in my bed."

"Meow." Oliver trotted toward him.

Jake swore under his breath as he backed away, then startled when Jess's hand touched his back. "You're as stealthy as a cat."

She barked a short laugh "I can be. When I'm not tripping over something. Did you and Oliver get things worked out?"

"You heard that?"

"I did. And I definitely cannot guarantee that he'll keep his distance. He's a lover not a fighter."

When he turned from eyeing the cat and got a good look at Jessica, he was speechless.

Speaking of lovers. Wow.

Her hair was in loose waves just begging to be tousled, and her pale-green dress was silky and feminine. He wanted to take her into his arms and kiss her on their way to the closest bed, or any other soft surface. Maybe even the kitchen counter. If only they could be casual lovers. But that was not what their relationship was about. Taking her to bed would complicate things between them. Too bad consummating their marriage or enjoying extra physical benefits hadn't been written into their Recipe for a Fake Marriage. But from his experience, most women weren't very good at casual sex.

Who am I kidding? I'm not good at it, either.

"Jake?"

"What?" He met her eyes and could tell she was fighting a smile and realized he'd been staring at her. All of her, from her shiny hair to her bright pink toenails.

"Are you ready to go or did you want to hang around here and—"

"We should go," he rushed to say before she finished that statement. He wasn't sure he wanted to know what she'd been planning to say next. Because if it had been anything close to intimate, he'd be hard-pressed to resist. "We don't want to be late." He turned for the door.

The front yard of Barton Estate had been transformed into a sea of flowers and candles and white fabric. Moments after arriving, Emma called Jessica over to see something on a long table.

Jake could hear them discussing the beauty of the decorations and how romantic it all was. His chest grew tight. His first wedding had been small and nothing fancy. When he and Jess eloped, it wouldn't even be a real wedding. They'd just stand before a judge in a courtroom and that would be that. It would be fake. A sham that got them what they both needed to fulfill career dreams and family obligations. But would it give them what they wanted? Suddenly, his heart ached for Jess. She deserved something real and beautiful.

"What are you thinking about so hard?" Anson said.

"Nothing much." *Liar, liar, pants on fire.*

"Are you starting to think about taking a trip down the aisle soon yourself?"

If he said he was thinking about marriage, it wouldn't be such a shock when they eloped. But the rumor might spread and someone, like his mother, might try to talk them out of it. Before he could make up his mind about how to answer, Luke joined them.

"The groom tapped one of the kegs behind the bar and said there is no need to wait for the reception," Luke said.

"Are you sure?" Anson did not look convinced. "The bride isn't going to mind if guests are drinking beer when she walks down the aisle?"

Luke shrugged. "We should probably put our glasses away before the wedding march starts."

Jake chuckled. "You think?" He turned to watched Jess. As if she'd felt him watching, she glanced over her shoulder. Her lovely face seemed to glow as her soft smile transformed into an expression that he'd swear held real feelings. She turned her body to face him, like an invitation to be part of her life.

If he was staying, he could see himself falling in love. He returned her smile, but his chest tightened painfully. He could not go down that thought path or give up what he'd worked so hard for. Years of training and effort could not be tossed away. Not to mention Jessica's rule about dangerous jobs.

Jessica straightened a floral arrangement on one of the tables, then took a seat beside Jake on the groom's side of the aisle. The sweet scent of flowers mingled with his spicy aftershave and made her sway in his direction.

"Have I told you how beautiful you look?" Jake rested his arm across the back of her chair.

His warm hand on her shoulder sent lovely little sparks dancing across her skin. "You have, but I don't mind a repeat."

A happy but nervous-looking groom took his place beside the preacher, and Jessica turned to see the wedding party gathered in front of the grand house.

"Is that the groom's daughter Emma is holding?" she whispered to Jake. Pink leg braces were visible above her ruffly socks and a tiny pair of white Mary Janes.

"Yes. That's Lilly. She often uses a gait trainer to help her walk, but the other kids are going to help her walk down the aisle. Lilly wants it to be a surprise for her daddy."

"Oh my gosh." She pressed her hands to her heart. "That is so sweet."

The soft background music changed, and the small wedding party took their places at the end of the flower-lined aisle.

"It's time," Hannah shouted and tossed a handful of pastel rose petals into the air, then received cheers and applause from the guests.

Emma set Lilly on her feet between Hannah and Cody, the shy little boy who'd hidden behind his mom at the diner. The trio started down the aisle, keeping a slow pace and supporting their friend with every step. Lilly's uneven gait and beaming smile were some of the most touching things Jessica had ever seen. Her heart squeezed at the care and tenderness among the three children.

As they neared the end of the aisle, Lilly giggled. "I did it, Daddy."

Brushing away a tear and clearly too emotional to speak, he picked up his daughter, held her close and kissed the top of her head. Rather than putting her down or handing her off to the maid of honor, Eric continued to hold his daughter.

Everyone was dabbing tears as they stood for the gorgeous, glowing bride who started down the aisle, escorted by her grandmother.

Gazing between the bride and groom, Jessica felt as if she could reach out and touch the love between them. She hung on every word of the ceremony and was hyper aware of Jake's finger tracing slow circles on her shoulder. If she was a cat, she'd be purring.

"I do," Eric said before the preacher could finish his sentence.

"I do, too," Lilly said with another adorable giggle, then leaned in her daddy's arms to kiss her new momma.

"And I do, too," Jenny said.

"I now pronounce you husband and wife and daughter."

Smiles, laughter and awes filled the evening like joyful music.

A tear trickled down Jessica's cheek, and Jake held her a little closer. Witnessing this union—more touching than any she'd ever seen—filled Jessica's heart with...hope. She'd never realized just how much she wanted this kind of love in her life. She wanted a man to look at her and pledge his life and love. She risked a glance at Jake, and when their eyes locked, her heart fluttered.

Is there a chance I can have this kind of love with Jake?

Maybe it was the romance of the evening, but in that moment, Jessica decided she was done being what her aunt called a worrywart. The future wasn't written in permanent ink, and it was time to treat the present as a gift and enjoy life. She'd deal with the aftereffects of their fake marriage… Well, after,

At least she wouldn't be blindsided by the end of their agreement.

After the bride and groom were congratulated and the food had been served, it was time for dancing.

Jake held out a hand to Jessica. "Dance with me?"

"I would love to."

The song was slow, and the dance floor was crowded, so they did little more than sway in one another's arms. Feeling inspired by her new positive outlook, she slipped her fingers into the back of his hair and would swear that the ocean of his blue eyes deepened. His lips brushed hers in a kiss so soft it was almost a dream, and she forgot to breathe.

I can "date" a guy and keep it casual, even if he is my fake husband.

As they drove up to her cabin, Jessica gazed at a moon that was almost full. "The stars are beautiful tonight. Want to sit on the side deck for a while before you go home?"

"Sounds good."

She kicked off her sandals and walked barefoot onto the porch. "That was the most emotional wedding I've ever been to. Especially when the children walked down the aisle. So much love."

"I liked it when Lilly said, 'I do.' And it got me thinking." Jake stepped in front of her and took her hands in his. "Jessica Talbot, will you elope with me on Wednesday? It's my day off."

It wasn't the marriage proposal of her dreams, but his crooked grin made her heart flutter.

"Well, seeing that it's your day off, how can I refuse such an offer?"

He brought her hand to his lips and kissed her knuckles. "For you, I would take the whole week off."

"Such a charmer." She cradled his cheek and let her fingers trail slowly along his five-o'clock shadow. And loved the flare in his eyes.

"If we spend one night, can you find someone to feed the cat and raccoons?" he asked.

"I bet Doc Ty will take the raccoons for a night, and I have an electronic feeding bowl for Ollie." "I know a hotel you'll love. It's called the Menger and has been in San Antonio since 1859. And they say it's haunted."

"How could a place that old not be?"

"That doesn't bother you?"

"No. It sounds exciting."

But not as exciting as becoming your wife...even if it is only pretend.

Chapter Fifteen

The spring afternoon was overcast and humid, but Jessica's mood was sunny. She'd worked in the morning and gone with Jake to the neighboring town on his lunch break to acquire a marriage license, and now it was time for shopping.

One look around the town square put a smile on her face. A young woman was watering the hanging baskets and potted plants in front of her shop. The air was filled with the mingling scents of fresh bread baking and flowers. A toddler giggled as his mom pushed his swing higher and higher. The sweet sound reminded her of Lilly's excitement when her friends helped her walk down the aisle.

Jenny and Eric's lovely outdoor wedding and Jake's elopement proposal were the inspiration for this morning's shopping trip. Their courthouse wedding would just be the two of them and a few strangers, but Jessica wanted something pretty and special to wear. The thought of just pulling something out of her closet made her sad, but because their elopement had to remain a secret, she'd be shopping alone for her secret wedding dress.

She crossed the street to the shop Emma had inherited from her late grandmother. Business partners, Emma and the newly married Jenny McKnight, were giving the shop a makeover, mixing vintage finds with Jenny's one-of-a kind designs. The store would become Emma's Vintage & Creations by Jenny. The new name required a new sign, and Alexandra, the artist of the group, was working on a design and logo.

Jessica adored the way this group of women cheered one another along. That type of support had not always been the case for her. Not when she was the rich kid at school or when she became an adult and people used her for her name and connections. The way this group of friends had accepted her was added proof she'd made the right decision to blow her entire savings on a down payment and move to Oak Hollow.

She returned the waves from an elderly couple she didn't yet know, then stopped in front of Emma's. Long plate-glass windows flanked the door. The displays were artfully arranged and so much more than just advertising, and they could stand up to the standards of a Beverly Hills boutique. The fashion was classic and elegant but still modern and wearable. It was hard to tell which were well-cared-for vintage pieces, and which were something Jenny had designed, but she couldn't wait to find out.

She walked into the shop she'd come to with Emma on those long-ago summers and learned about mixing old and new in her wardrobe. Since it was a weekday, she knew Emma would be teaching school, and Jenny would no doubt be on her honeymoon, but the sign said Open. She was surprised when Jenny greeted her.

"I didn't expect to see you here today," Jessica said.

Her smile was bright and shiny just as a new bride's should be. "We had the house to ourselves on our wedding night and have a longer honeymoon planned for next week. Are you just stopping in to visit or shopping?"

"Both. I need a new summery dress that is on the dressier side."

"I can definitely help you out with that."

"I'm so long-waisted that it's hard to find dresses with a waistband that doesn't end up across my rib cage."

Jenny held up and wiggled a finger like she was dinging a bell. "I can fix that problem."

"Awesome." She heard little girls giggling and saw the precious faces of the star flower girls, Hannah and Lilly, peeking around a display shelf. "Hello, you two."

"Come see," Hannah said.

Behind the shelf, there was a child-size table set for a pretend tea party. "This looks like so much fun."

"You can play, too," Lilly said.

"Can I shop for a new dress first?"

The little girls looked at one another, then nodded. "Okay."

Jenny chuckled. "Let's start over here." She led her to a rack across the back wall. A row of silky dresses hung in a pastel rainbow of soft fabrics. "This silk and chiffon might be fancier than you want, but I think the style and fit are something you'll like."

"That pale pink is beautiful." She couldn't tell her new friend that the fabric was perfect for a wedding, even if it was at the county courthouse.

"It's called whisper pink." Jenny pulled a dress from the rack. "This style doesn't have a defined waistband, plus I can take in a few gathers and tailor it to you. If you like it, of course."

"It's gorgeous. I definitely want to try it on."

Jenny checked the size, then led her to a dressing room. "Start with this and I'll grab a few more."

Jessica looked at the price tag, relieved it wasn't priced like it would be if it were in a shop in Beverly Hills. She was supposed to be saving money, not spending it. When the smooth fabric slid softly against her skin, her thoughts veered into daydream territory involving Jake's touch and silk sheets.

A girl could dream.

She met her reflection and butterflies spiraled through her belly. "Oh, I love this dress." The halter-style flowed into a princess seam waistline and then to layers of silk and chiffon in a handkerchief hemline to midcalf.

"Can we see?" one of the little girls called to her.

Jessica smiled at her reflection. She'd been a little bummed about doing this all alone. But she wasn't alone. She had people waiting to see her in this beautiful dress. "Here I come." She stepped out of the dressing room and swished the skirt to the delight of both girls.

"Oooh. Pretty," Lilly said and wiggled her little walker in excitement.

"Thank you. I love it, too. This is exactly what I was looking for."

"You a bootiful bride," Hannah exclaimed and clapped her hands.

Jessica's breath caught. How did this sweet little child know? She glanced toward a full-length mirror.

Do I look like a bride?

"We can throw flowers in your wedding, too," Lilly said. "We have dresses."

Jessica cleared her throat and met their sweet smiling faces. "I saw you in your beautiful dresses and you did such a good job. Prettiest flower girls I've ever seen. I'm not having a wedding right now, but if I do, I'll be sure to let you both know."

The girls cheered.

Jenny came around the corner with more dresses and hung them on a hook. "That looks fabulous on you."

"I absolutely love it." Jessica swished the skirt once more.

"Oh, good. Let's see if I need to adjust anything."

She ended up buying the first one she'd tried on and had a celebratory tea party with Hannah and Lilly. Jessica then picked up food from the Acorn Cafe and took it over to Jake's dad. Once Jake got home, the three of them ate together, like a family.

They had acquired a marriage license and Jake had booked a hotel room. And this beautiful woman riding beside him would be his wife before the end of the day.

Your pretend wife.

He'd had to remind himself of that fact several times over the last few days.

About halfway to San Antonio, they stopped at an antique store to deliver a dresser that was part of a trade between Tess and the owner. After he helped someone unload it, he found Jessica by the register, bent at the waist, and intently looking at something in a glass jewelry case.

Jake came up beside her and mimicked her position. "What did you find?"

"Just checking out the antique jewelry."

A plump elderly woman behind the counter pulled out the tray of rings and set it before them. "Feel free to try them on." A phone rang in the little office across the hall. "I need to get that. Be right back."

Jake picked up a plain gold band and examined it. "We should have rings. People will expect us to have rings. Won't they?" *Why didn't I think of this?*

"Probably, but we can just say that it was so spur of the moment that we didn't have a chance."

"But don't women always ask to see one another's rings?"

"I guess having a ring will prevent questions. We need to make this marriage look as real as possible, so no one suspects."

When Jess touched one with a large pale blue stone, his throat tightened. *Oh, crap.* He couldn't afford that today. Not until they were married, and she could access her trust fund money. Then he'd get his loan. "Is that blue stone some kind of diamond?"

She lifted her hand without picking up the ring, and he caught her soft wistful sigh. And it made his heart catch.

"No. It's an aquamarine." She smiled at him. "It matches your eyes. Let's just get a couple of simple bands. That's enough to get the message across."

"We have time and there are options right in front of us." He tried on a gold band, but it was too small to go over his knuckle.

She handed him another. "Try this one. It looks a little bigger." It slid on and fit perfectly.

The woman returned to the counter. "Did you find anything you like?"

"I did," he said. "Now, we need one for…my fiancée." His heart gave an extra strong thump against his breastbone.

"What will match your—" The woman cut off her words when she looked at Jessica's left hand as if expecting to see an engagement ring. She picked up the aquamarine, which was likely the most expensive ring in the store and held it out to Jessica. "Try this one."

"That's probably too much."

"Well, just try it for size. I know it's a size six."

Jess hesitated before taking it, slipped it on her finger, stared at it a moment and then took it off. "The size is perfect, but a simple gold band like his is what I need.

But what ring does she want*? Jake wondered.*

He wanted to pull her into a hug, but instead they reached for the same ring and their hands touched, sending a jolt up his arm.

That one fit her perfectly, and they left with two golden wedding bands. But not before he caught Jessica glancing a few more times at the blue stone. He wished he could buy it for her, but their arrangement was not about fancy rings.

They drove straight to the hotel to check in and change clothes. Standing at the front desk, Jessica seemed nervous, so he put his arm around her because he was feeling the same way.

The woman at the front desk smiled and welcomed them. "Are you here for a special occasion? Anniversary or birthday?"

"We're getting married today," Jake said.

"Congratulations."

"The reservation is for Jake Carter."

She looked at the computer screen. "This room won't do at all. I'm going to upgrade you to the perfect room, and it will be at no extra charge. One of the perks of being a manager," she said and winked. "We love to help guests celebrate special moments."

Jake had booked a room with two beds, and he had a feeling the one she'd switched them to would not, but he couldn't very well say he needed two beds in his honeymoon suite.

"Thank you," Jake and Jessica said in unison.

When he opened the door to their room, the first thing he saw was one king-size bed located in the middle of the space like a flashing beacon. Neither of them mentioned that fact but both of their gazes shot that way.

Jake hung her garment bag in the tiny closet and glanced at his watch. "Our appointment is in three hours. All I need is a quick shower and to change my clothes."

"I need a shower, too." With her shoes kicked off, she sat on the foot of the bed. The one and only bed.

Focus, dude.

"If I can get ready first, I'll be quick," he said. "I need to run down to the lobby for something and you can get ready in private."

"Sure. You go ahead. I'll enjoy this gorgeous room. It's so elegant and luxurious." With her legs still dangling off the edge of the tall bed, she lay back with her arms spread wide. "And I need some time to cool off."

He needed to cool off, too, because the vision of her position on the bed was heating him up hotter than an August day in Texas. If he hooked his hands under her knees and pulled her hips forward, she'd be at the perfect height to—

Whoa. Stop it.

He rubbed his eyes, then grabbed what he needed and went into the bathroom where he took a cold shower. When he stepped out dressed in black slacks and a pale-gray button up, she was gathering things from her suitcase.

"Wow. You look very handsome."

"Thanks." The way she was looking at him was either going to make him blush or need another cold shower. "Call me if you think of anything you need while I'm out?"

"I have everything I need," she said before he closed the door.

As he got on the elevator, Jake replayed her words: *I have everything I need.*

Did he have everything he needed?

After a shower, Jessica did her hair and makeup, then slipped on her dress. Jenny was an amazing designer, and she felt lucky to have one of her creations. It made her feel confident and feminine. With one more glance in the mirror, she stepped out into the hotel room.

Jake turned from the window and the tension that had creased his forehead softened as he smiled in a way that made his blue eyes dance. In this moment, she felt like the most beautiful woman in the world.

It was a sparkly sensation she'd hold on to and re-member forever.

"You look amazingly beautiful."

"Thank you."

From the dresser, he grabbed a bouquet of pink and white roses with the stems wrapped in satin ribbon. "I got these for you. They go well with your dress."

Every part of her sighed with pleasure. "They're gorgeous. I love them."

"Every bride should have a bouquet."

She brought the flowers to her nose, letting the fresh scent fill her. "How did you get a bouquet in such a short time?"

"I had some help from the manager who checked us in."

"You keep surprising me, Jake Carter. In good ways."

This man is one of the good ones. Too bad he's not mine to keep.

They arrived at the courthouse twenty minutes before their scheduled time and waited on a bench in the hallway. His hands clenched and unclenched, and with the sleeves of his pale-gray shirt rolled up to midforearm, she could admire the movement of his muscles. It touched her heart that he seemed nervous, because so was she.

When it was their turn, her pulse began to race, and she trembled.

Jake gently tucked her hair behind her ear, then took her hand. "I've got you, Mystery Woman."

His voice was soft and filled with kindness and most of her nervousness drifted away. "I'm ready."

The ceremony, if you could even call it that, was short and to the point. And she was so focused on Jake's handsome face she barely heard what was said.

"I now pronounce you husband and wife. You may kiss the bride," the female judge said with a bright smile.

Jake cupped one side of her face, and when their lips met and sparks danced between them, she wrapped her arms around his waist and held tight.

"So sweet," he whispered as he raised his head.

In a matter of minutes, she'd become someone's wife. They were married, but in name only. Unless…

Would living in the same house lead to more?

They ate dinner at a nice restaurant on the River Walk, saw some of the sights and then went back to their hotel, where there was only one bed. He slid the keycard through the slot and opened the door, but they just stood there. He was no doubt waiting for her to walk in first, but she held out a little hope that he'd carry her over the threshold, like he'd done in her kitchen when he'd thought she'd pass out.

I'm expecting too much. She took a step to go inside.

"Wait," Jake said and caught her arm. "We did the rings and flowers, so…" He scooped her into his arms and walked through the doorway.

Jessica laughed as a pleasant shiver rippled across her, and the grin on his face told her he'd felt it.

A bottle of champagne on ice along with strawberries and whipped cream were arranged on the dresser.

"Did you do this?" they both asked at the same time, then laughed before he set her on her feet.

"It must be the manager," he said. "We need to give her a glowing review."

"For sure."

Now that they were alone in their hotel room, they were suddenly acting as shy as teenagers on their very first date. It could be the wine they'd shared at dinner. It could be the big soft bed.

But most likely, it was the feelings that were growing between them.

Needing a moment alone to give herself a cautionary talking-to, she pulled a set of black silk pajamas from her suitcase. "I'm going to change, and then what do you say we pop open this champagne?"

"Good plan."

In their pajamas on the big bed, they drank champagne and talked about the summers she'd spent in Oak Hollow, surprised that they'd each had a crush on the other but been too shy to do anything about it. Late into the night they laughed, and there was no mistaking the tenderness between them. They drifted into sleep with their bodies so close their legs were touching.

Jessica woke in the night with Jake spooned behind her, his arm cradling her against his chest. She snuggled deeper into his strong, warm embrace, soaking up every second of this new feeling. A feeling she dared not put a name to. This was another moment in time she'd commit to memory.

The time a wonderful man made her feel beautiful and special.

His breathing changed and his fingers flexed against her stomach before sliding to her hip, but she held perfectly still, not wanting him to know she was awake. Not wanting him to roll away and leave her alone.

"Jess." His voice was barely a whisper, and he nuzzled his face against the back of her neck.

Delicious little shivers rippled from the spot his lips touched her skin. Unable to resist, she turned in his arms and raised her face to his, their lips so close there was no fighting the pull. This time, it was so much more than a gentle press of lips. The kiss was deep and warm and all-consuming in the best way possible.

His strong hands roamed over her silk pajamas, leaving trails of fiery pleasure, but never slipping under to touch her skin. And still, it was the most erotic connection of her life.

Tonight, they held one another. But tomorrow… What would come with the morning light?

Chapter Sixteen

Jake woke before dawn with that momentary sense of confusion and played it off as a dream, but the warmth and scent of the woman beside him was real. This might not be his bed or room, but the woman in his arms was… His wife.

It all came flooding back. The courthouse wedding. Laughing together with a bottle of champagne and strawberries. Falling asleep in the same bed and wishing he could make love to her. And then…waking in the night, his willpower had vanished when she'd turned in his arms. They'd made out like teenagers before drifting back to sleep.

It was still too dark to see her, but his other senses were fully awake. Heat pooled low in his body, but also filled his heart. This might be the only night with Jess, and he wanted more. He filled his lungs with her honeysuckle scent.

She responded almost immediately, arching against him. Her soft hands set fire to his body with every caress. Every brush of her sweet lips and warm tongue. Every breathy sigh and erotic movement. He kissed her with all the passion and fireworks a wedding night should have. And without having sex, he made love to his pretend wife. They might not have consummated their marriage in the traditional sense, but his heart was branded, and he craved his mystery woman.

With her lovely body curled against his chest, he was getting ideas about being more than friends. He was married to a woman he wanted more with every day.

Why can't I have her? He sighed, knowing the answer to his question. *Because I have to protect her.*

It wouldn't be fair to start something real and then leave her behind when he moved. She'd made it clear from the start that she did not want a long-term relationship with a police officer. And even though that made him sad, he'd respect it.

After breakfast in the dining room of their hotel, they drove out of downtown San Antonio, and the traffic was bumper to bumper. He was not looking forward to returning to the congested Dallas traffic. But he loved his job there. He loved working with dogs and the guys in the K9 unit. He had the chance for a great promotion that shouldn't be passed up.

Jake couldn't stop sneaking glances at Jess. If it was only his feelings to consider, he'd kiss her again and see if she wanted him as much as he did her. But it wasn't only him. He'd never had a friendship like this with a woman, and he valued their connection and didn't want to screw it up. If they took things to a more intimate level...

Would it ruin everything? He glanced at her, and she smiled in a way that grabbed hold of him. *Maybe we could—* He had to stop thinking with his libido.

"How are we going to tell everyone that we got married?" she asked.

Focus, dude.

"We can ask everyone over for a barbecue and tell them all at once."

"Oh, yes. That way, we don't have to go through the explanation over and over. And since we will be in a big group, hopefully everyone will mind their manners and not say anything negative in front of other people," Jessica said.

He glanced at his watch. "I think tonight is too soon."

"It is. Especially since we need to make one stop before we get home. I have a surprise for you."

"You do? What is it?"

"I'd rather show you." She pulled up directions on her phone. "I'll tell you where to turn."

"Okay."

Off a county road, they turned onto a long drive-way that led to Coleman Ranch. Jake sucked in a breath when he saw the sign that announced dog breeding.

"Surprise," she said. "I know there's no guarantee that you'll find the right puppy today, but I picked this place after doing some research and discovering the Colemans are known for well-bred dogs. They have a reputation for clean spacious areas for the animals and superb animal treatment."

"You did all that for me?" His heart suddenly felt too big for his chest.

"I did."

"Have I told you you're amazing?"

"No." A pink flush bloomed on her cheeks. "But I like hearing it. I've already told them all about you, your job and your training credentials. You're preapproved."

They were met by a sweet older couple who proudly showed them around their facilities. Jake breathed a sigh of relief that it was not the kind of puppy mill he'd heard horror stories about. Just as Jess had said, all of the animals had plenty of space, there were no cages and everything was fresh and clean. The couple took them out to a large, fenced area where mother dogs and their puppies played in the sunshine or slept in the shade of several large trees.

"We have five German shepherd puppies, one chocolate Lab and three yellow Labs," the man said.

"I'm interested in the shepherd puppies," Jake said.

"Why don't you go in alone first and see which ones interact with you." Mr. Coleman started unlatching the gate. "We've found that a dog and their person will often connect with one another quickly."

Jake liked that attitude and entered the fenced area alone and was immediately greeted by an excited group of wiggling little pups. He kneeled on the grass and allowed the puppies to inspect him as much as he did them.

After most of the puppies ran off to play, a little female German shepherd stayed by his side. She sat on the grass but leaned against him. Jake glanced over his shoulder and smiled at Jess. "Come inside and see this little lady." He valued her professional opinion, but the truth was, he just wanted to share the moment with her.

She came through the gate and kneeled beside them, and the puppy rolled over for a tummy rub. "She has flower petals stuck in her hair."

Mrs. Coleman pointed to a patch of daisies in the flower bed along the front of her house. "We had a family here this morning and the little boy let this one out. She ran straight for my flowers and had a good roll around in the daisies. The family ended up wanting a male dog."

"I'm glad they didn't take her because she is the one I want," Jake said. "How old is she?"

"She turned eight weeks yesterday," said Mrs. Coleman. "Shall I start the paperwork?"

"Yes, please." He picked up his new puppy, and she tried to lick his face.

"You should name her Daisy," Jess said.

"I don't know about that."

* * *

Once they had stopped for pet supplies and were back on the road toward home, Jessica sent a group text to their friends inviting them to a barbecue the next evening.

"Are you okay with stopping to tell Pops in person before we go to your ranch?"

"Of course. Telling him will be a good test of how people might respond. What about your mom?"

Jake groaned and made a face. "Do we have to?"

She laughed without any real joy and turned up the song on the radio. "I think we do. I barely know her, but I get the feeling she's the kind of woman who might already know, and then we'll be in trouble."

"Well, let's not do it tonight."

"Agreed. Do you think people will now assume you aren't taking the job in Dallas?"

"Pops and Anson would like for me to stay in Oak Hollow."

"Not your mother. I know because she told me about it almost first thing."

"Somehow, that doesn't surprise me."

"Hey, Pops," Jake called out as they walked in the door. "I'm home with a new family member." The puppy barked, and he put her down. She ran a lap around the couch, then wiggled at his dad's feet.

"Hello there. Aren't you a cute pup?" Pops rubbed her head and lifted her into his lap. "Is this why you went to San Antonio?"

"No. The puppy is an extra perk." His mouth grew

suddenly dry. Jake wrapped his arm around Jessica's waist. "Actually, I brought home two new family members." They held up their left hands, showing off their gold wedding bands.

His dad's mouth dropped open wide enough to catch flies. He squinted as he studied them. "Are y'all messing with me?"

"No."

Pops smiled, then stood and put the puppy down. "Dang, son, you only had to go on a date to win our bet about the paint color."

"I wanted to be sure." Jake laughed, happy with his dad's response to their news. But at the same time, he felt horrible for deceiving him.

"I can't say your marriage isn't a big surprise, but I can see the love between you two."

Jess flinched against Jake's side, but he didn't dare look at her and risk his dad noticing anything.

"Congratulations." He drew them both into a hug. "Welcome to the family."

"Thank you," Jessica said and wiped a tear from the corner of her eye.

"Son, I knew you were smart. I'm glad you married this woman before she got away."

When Jess went into the bathroom, Pops motioned for Jake to follow him into the kitchen, and the puppy trotted along behind them. "Does your mother know about this yet?"

"No. You're the first to know."

"Are you going to call her?" His furrowed brow

expressed his understanding of how difficult the conversation would be.

Jake rubbed both hands up and down his face. "Yes. At some point. I'm just not looking forward to the lecture."

"I understand. Want me to call her?"

Before they could finish the conversation, Jess joined them. "Should we take the puppy out before we get back in the truck?"

"Good idea," he said. The puppy ran around in the backyard where he'd played as a kid. "Do we need to go pick up the raccoons?"

"No. I texted Doc Ty, and he said to leave them until tomorrow." She rubbed the pup's fuzzy tummy. "I still think you should name her Daisy."

"You really want me to name a police dog after a flower?"

"Why not?" She grinned "Daisy? Are you a good girl?"

The puppy barked, and her little tail took off at a full speed wag.

"See, she likes the name. Go stand over there and test out a few names. See what she responds to."

He crossed the yard to humor Jessica. "Come here, Fido. Spot, come girl." He got no response. "Daisy, come girl."

The puppy spun around and barreled his way.

"Well, damn." When he met his wife's beautiful smile, his heart lit up.

The sun was setting as they drove up to her cabin, spreading brilliant colors across the sky behind the river. It was like driving into a postcard, and Jessica still couldn't believe this ranch was hers. And now that she was married, she would be able to keep it. She glanced at her pretend husband and got the same tingly feeling she always did. Her property might be safe... But would she be able to keep her heart intact?

The answer was a big fat no. She'd already let him in. But as she'd told herself at Jenny and Eric's wedding, she'd enjoy the present and tend to her heartache later.

Daisy was asleep in her puppy crate, but she woke when Jake got her out of the car. He clipped on her leash and walked her around the front yard, trying out a few simple commands. Once everything had been brought inside, and the cat and dog had met with only a bit of hesitation on both sides, Jake and Jessica stood in the kitchen, unsure what to do next.

"I really enjoyed our trip," she said and poured water into the coffeemaker.

"Me, too. Sorry we couldn't stay longer to see more of the town."

"There's plenty of time for that. How about we take a shower and then watch that movie we were talking about?"

"You're inviting me to take a shower?" His lips twitched.

"Oh! I..." She laughed. "I didn't mean together."
But damn if it isn't a very tempting idea.

"I know. I like teasing you because you get the cutest little dimple right here." He stepped closer and brushed his finger over her cheek.

His nearness and touch made her want to drag him to her shower whether it was a good idea or not.

Once they had showered—alone in separate bathrooms—Jessica found Jake sitting in her overstuffed chair with a sleeping puppy on his lap. Not on the couch where there was the possibility of her sitting beside him. There would be no snuggling tonight. Their wonderful wedding night had probably been her one shot at that, and it was a good thing she had committed it to memory.

"I've got the movie cued up," he said.

"Excellent. Go ahead and start it." With a long inner sigh, she settled on the couch and Oliver came over to join her. At least there was one male who couldn't resist her. Too bad he was feline. Even though she'd known this was how it would be, after their closeness in San Antonio, she'd foolishly allowed herself to hold out hope that Jake would find her irresistible. Feeling suddenly cold inside, she pulled the fluffy throw off the back of the couch.

She should've suggested watching a comedy instead of the action drama that she hadn't known would revolve around a bad relationship and dredge up the past. While the movie played, Jessica's mind kept revisiting a memory that held embarrassment and a wound that was yet to heal. The memory of a college boyfriend who'd told her she was too vanilla and boring in bed.

Is that why Jake was having no problem sitting across the room from her?

I just want to be desired.

Jake had fallen asleep in the chair with the snooz-ing puppy curled up on his lap. With his features re-laxed, he looked adorable. So handsome and such a good man. And she couldn't be the reason he gave up on a career he loved.

A job that comes with too much risk.

Oliver yawned, stretched, hopped off the couch and crept toward Jake and Daisy. Jessica stood to stop him before he woke them and freaked out the big tough police officer. The thought made her chuckle and she stood back to watch while Oliver silently leaped up onto the stuffed arm of the chair and stared at the sleeping pair.

They all needed a good night's sleep, but the puppy needed one more trip outside before sleep-ing in her crate. Jessica started to lift her from his lap, but like a good doggy dad, his hand came up to cradle the pup. But he clasped her hand instead.

I wish he'd never let go.

Jake woke when his new puppy wiggled on his lap. Without opening his eyes, he reached to hold her before she could jump onto the floor and make a mess. But instead of his hand meeting hair, he felt soft skin and, on a sharp inhale, the scent of hon-eysuckle. His eyes flew open to find Jessica lean-ing over him, and for a moment, he thought she was going to kiss him.

And he wanted her to. Their gazes met and held for a heated moment.

Jess remained still and did not pull her hand away from his. "I was going to take Daisy outside and didn't want to wake you."

He was awake now. All of him. He had gone from asleep to fully alert in seconds. But that's when he noticed the cat sitting on the arm of his chair, just inches from him and staring like he was a tasty treat.

Jessica slid her hand from under his and lifted her cat, barely restraining a smile.

Looks like he'd need to make friends with Oliver. "I'll take Daisy out."

"Daisy? I'm so glad you've taken my naming advice," Jess said with a huge grin.

"Y'all ganged up on me." He gathered his puppy into his arms and headed for the door. Hopefully some cool night air would help subdue his suddenly overactive sex drive.

Daisy did her business quickly, but Jake wasn't ready to go back inside. Last night they'd had no choice but to sleep in the same bed. But tonight… he'd have to sleep down the hallway, knowing what it was like to hold her against his chest.

Daisy sat on his foot and leaned against his leg. He lifted his tiny puppy and held her in front of his face. "What are we going to do about this situation we've gotten ourselves into?"

The puppy gave a little growl, then yipped as if to say, *I didn't get us into this. That was all you, buddy.*

Chapter Seventeen

While sitting on the deck with a cup of morning coffee, Jessica dialed her aunt's number. After the usual hellos and such, she prepared to break the news.

"So, remember I told you about dating Jake? The guy I had a crush on years ago."

"Yes. How is that going?"

"Great." Jessica took a deep breath. "In fact, so great that…we eloped."

"You what?"

Aunt Kay's voice rose to a shrill level that had Jessica pulling the phone from her ear. "I know this is superfast, but it felt right. He's not like any other guy I've dated, and I think my dad would've really liked him."

"Wow. When I encouraged you to start dating,

I had no idea you'd take me so seriously. And so quickly. I didn't even get to help you plan a wedding." Kay cleared her throat. "Did you do this so you could—"

"I'm so glad I took your advice," Jessica said, cutting her off before she asked *the question*. Was it about the trust fund money? Unable to sit still, she got up from her chair and moved to the railing. "I made myself take a leap and I'm so happy. And I have you to thank for giving me the push I needed. I suppose I also owe thanks to my father for adding this strange stipulation to the trust. Without it, I never would've put myself out there." Her stomach knotted more with every fib she told.

"But why did you elope? You haven't had time to get pregnant."

"Aunt Kay! It's not because I'm pregnant."

Once her aunt's voice had returned to a normal volume, she got her talked down to acceptance and then happiness. But the whole phone call left her mentally exhausted and made her even more glad Jake wanted to wait to tell the very opinionated Jewels Carter. However, there was only so long they could put it off.

Jake stepped out onto the deck and leaned on the railing beside her. "How did it go?"

"It went about like I expected. She was shocked, then suspicious but finally landed on happiness" Having Jake beside her, close enough to feel the heat of his arm, calmed her. "I'm glad we told Pops first. His response was good. How do you think everyone will react tonight? Emma is the only one I know well enough to guess."

"I think they'll be surprised but supportive and happy for us," he said.

"Good. Well, we have about a dozen people coming over tonight. I need to go get the raccoons from Doc Ty and help him with something. If I give you a list, will you go buy stuff for the barbecue?"

"Sure. There's a great butcher shop on the square."

"Thanks." She gave him a quick kiss on the mouth, then held her breath, and he seemed to do the same. Her lips tingled and so did her nerves. She hadn't meant to do it. It had just come naturally. "I'd better go get dressed." She rushed into the house and pressed her fingertips to her mouth, wanting to kiss him again, and this time, not stop at one quick kiss.

Before sunset, Tess, Anson and Hannah arrived with homemade potato salad.

"Where are the babies?" Hannah asked before she was two steps into the house.

Jessica shared a smile with her parents. "The baby raccoons are in my room in their kennel. Would you like to see them?"

"Yes, pease." Hannah clapped her little hands and bounced from foot to foot.

After a supervised visit with Loki and Floki, Hannah played outside with Daisy and became their official greeter as more guests arrived. The adults watched from the deck as Hannah welcomed Alexandra, Luke and her friend Cody. Lilly, who had stolen everyone's hearts at the wedding, was the next child to arrive with her newly married parents, Eric and Jenny. Emma and Pops soon completed their guest list.

Her ranch was busy with activity and happy voices, and she realized this was what she'd been missing. With the enormous house she'd grown up in, she'd been used to lots of empty, quiet rooms. Jessica had enjoyed her own company and hadn't thought to change that, but now... Hearing their childish giggles struck a place in her heart, and Jessica couldn't help but think about what it would be like to have a child with Jake. To be a family and part of this group of friends.

It's going to be harder than I thought to watch him move away.

Needing a moment to get her emotions under control, Jessica stepped away from the group and watched the kids from the railing of her deck. Once Oliver took a few minutes to observe the three little people playing in the yard with Daisy, he crept out from under a lantana bush. Cody was sitting cross-legged in the grass and Oliver took it as an invitation to crawl into his lap. The little boy's smile grew as he stroked the big orange cat.

Jake came up behind her, wrapped his arms around her waist and drew her close against his chest. "Are you okay? You look so deep in thought."

Her heart instantly leaped at the feel of his embrace, but just as quickly she told herself his hug was for their guests' benefit. Regardless, she tipped her head back to rest on his shoulder and savored the moment. "I'm just marveling at Cody's bravery. He's risking life and limb with your feline nemesis."

Jake laughed and hugged her closer. "Is that an insinuation that I'm more of a chicken than a six-year-old?"

"Hey, you're the one who said it." Standing in the circle of his arms she decided that having people around was a very good thing. In their charade to appear as a couple in love, she was able to act on her desire to touch and kiss him whenever she wanted to. It was nice not to constantly fight the urge, and she suddenly wished Pops would move in with them.

"Want me to bring out the cheese and fruit platter?" Emma asked.

Without letting go of her, Jake turned them around.

"Yes, please," Jessica said.

"I guess we better tend to our guests and figure out when to break the news," he whispered against her ear.

She turned in his arms, and when his pupils dilated, she kissed him. A soft brush of lips, then once more, and ending with a harder press that made him moan. "Everyone is watching us"

"Who cares." He stole his own kiss before they rejoined their guests.

Jessica and Jake were arranging food on the new patio table when someone gasped.

Rushing closer, Emma grabbed Jessica's left hand. "Oh my God! Do you two have on wedding rings?"

Instant silence overtook the patio. All Jessica

A MARRIAGE OF BENEFITS

could hear was the distant rushing river and the children's laughter. And her own heartbeat. Pops was grinning from ear to ear, but everyone else wore varying degrees of surprise.

Jake and Jessica shared a smile and held up their hands. "We sure do," he said. "We eloped while we were in San Antonio."

Now, everyone was talking at once. Some were hugging them with words of congratulations and others still looked confused. Any questions would likely come later when there weren't so many people around.

Jake brought out a bottle of champagne Jessica hadn't known about. "Where did that come from?"

"I bought it today so we could have a toast with everyone."

"Great idea." His thoughtfulness touched her heart and was definitely something she could get used to.

Jake popped the cork, and everyone cheered. He winked at Jessica and her heart got all melty like chocolate in the sunshine.

She let herself fall completely into the performance for the rest of the evening. And she wasn't having the least bit of trouble being convincing. It was the best performance of her life. Only problem was...it was no act.

I'm falling in love with my fake husband.

Chapter Eighteen

Jake had just pulled the police cruiser into the lot behind the station when his cell phone rang with a Dallas number.

"Hey, Captain Phillips. How are things?"

"Real good. Just calling to see how your dad is doing?"

"A little better every day." Although Jake was relieved Pops was pretty much back to his usual self and almost ready to go back to work, at the same time, it meant he could technically return to Dallas sooner than first thought. And leave Jessica. An empty feeling hit the pit of his stomach.

"Glad to hear he's improving," Captain Phillips said in his gruff voice. "Hope you aren't getting too comfortable in your hometown because I have good news for you. You know that promotion we talked about?"

"Yes."

"Well, I have an even better offer for you. Sullivan is taking an early retirement and wants you to be his replacement. And I agree."

"Honestly?" Excitement kicked up inside him. This was an even bigger promotion. A chance to do exactly what he wanted ahead of schedule. "I'm... Wow."

Captain Phillips laughed. "Everyone is looking forward to you coming home. Positions on First Squad don't come along every day."

Women like Jessica don't, either.

He'd think about that reaction later.

"He's not retiring for another three months, but that doesn't mean you can't come back before then. When do you think you'll be back up here?"

"I'll let you know a timeline soon," Jake said.

"Good deal. Talk to you later."

Jake ended the call and got out of the hot car. This was the promotion he'd been hoping for. It would allow him to do what he loved every day. A great job with great pay. If only it was in Oak Hollow.

Back inside the station, he was trying to figure out a way to tell everyone about his promotion.

"Heads up, Jake. Incoming," Anson said.

He spun around. "Oh, hell." His mother stormed in the front door of the police station. Someone had told her before he'd had a chance. Putting off telling her was a bad decision.

"You're in trouble now," Anson said under his breath. "Want to use my office?"

"Yeah. Thanks." He recognized the look on his mother's face. A full-strength hurricane was coming straight for him.

"Hi, Mom. I was planning to call you today."

With her hands on her hips, she shook her head but didn't say a word.

"Let's go into the chief's office."

She followed him inside, and the second he closed the door she let out a big sigh. "What in the world were you thinking?"

"About what?"

"You know good and well what." Her scowl was threatening to override her Botox.

"Who told you?"

"Your father called me. He thought he could smooth things over, but there is no smoothing this over. If you weren't a grown man, I'd spank you."

With his feet braced wide, he crossed his arms over his chest. "Well, as you just mentioned, I am a grown man and can make my own decisions."

She flung her hands in the air and dropped into a chair. "You are going to throw away your career for that girl?"

"That girl is my wife, and I'll not have you saying anything bad about her. And nobody said anything about throwing away a career."

"Is she going to sell her ranch and move to Dallas?"

"We're still working on that." He glanced at his

watch. "In about fifteen minutes I need to be at the rec center to teach a safety class. Can we talk about this later?"

"Well, since you don't have time to call or even talk to your mother in person, I'll go see your father. Maybe he can help me talk some sense into you." She left without another word.

Jake propped both hands on the desk and took a few deep breaths. Everything was snowballing. His fake relationship was way more difficult than he'd thought. But somewhere deep inside, he'd known it would be from the second he said, "I do." Taking a seat in Anson's chair, he called his dad.

"Sorry. I had to call her," Pops said in place of hello.

"Did you really?"

"If we had waited any longer, you know how upset she'd be."

"I'm not sure it could get much worse."

Since Jake was at work, Jessica took an emergency vet call for Doc Ty. She was updating the patient chart at his desk when her phone rang with an upbeat song that signaled Aunt Kay was calling.

"Hello. How's everyone in California?"

"All good. Remember my friend Tiffany?"

The excitement in her aunt's voice was unmistakable. "Yes. The one who just married the movie mogul."

"They have a private plane and are flying to Texas

to look at some property, and I'm tagging along so I can come see your new home."

Her pulse took a leap. "Oh, good."

Hopefully her voice and tone sounded sincere. Any other time she'd be thrilled at the prospect of her aunt's trip, but right now... With any luck, she wouldn't come within the next couple of weeks. She and Jake were just figuring out how to live in the same house. And she was adjusting to living with the off-limits man she had fallen for. How obvious would the truth be to her aunt who knew her so well?

"I have felt so bad about not getting to Texas to see you sooner. I hope you don't mind that I'm coming?" Her aunt rushed on without waiting for an answer. "I have so many things to catch up on. Seeing your new house, and most importantly, meeting your new husband."

Aha. This is an investigative checkup more than a visit.

No doubt Aunt Kay wanted to see for herself if Jessica had married just to get the money, which of course was exactly what she had done. But her aunt could never ever know the truth. "When are you coming?"

"I'm already on the way," Kay said in her big cheery voice. "We will be landing at a small private airport near Oak Hollow."

Jessica sprang up from the desk chair so fast it rolled into the wall hard enough to rattle framed photos. Her initial apprehension turned to panic. She didn't know what to say, but that was fine because her aunt continued talking while Jessica ran through a mental checklist of what needed to be done. And done soon. Like right now. She needed to better prepare her fake husband for the whirlwind that was Aunt Kay.

They'd have to share a bedroom while she was here. A very pleasant jolt ran through her body.

That part won't be so bad.

"I just found out about their trip," Kay continued, "and when Tiffany suggested I come along, I rushed to pack and get to the airport. It's only for one night but the timing is perfect. I didn't have time to call until now. Hope it's okay."

"Sure." What else was she supposed to say? "You are always welcome. What time do you think you'll arrive in Oak Hollow?"

"There's a rental car waiting for me at the airport, and I'll get to your house somewhere between one or two o'clock your time. And I'll be leaving tomorrow evening."

With a glance at her watch, Jessica's heart raced. She needed to get home in plenty of time to make sure everything appeared that they were happy newlyweds who were sharing a bedroom.

"I'm so excited to meet your new husband. See you soon, dear."

"Can't wait," she said and ended the call. She had a feeling her aunt had purposely waited to call so she couldn't say no to this pop-in inspection, but at least she hadn't shown up completely unannounced. Jessica dialed Jake, but her call went to voice mail, and too frazzled to think of what to say, she hung up.

Quickly finishing the patient chart, she skipped the errands she had planned and rushed home. Her aunt would need the room Jake had used the past two nights, and she only had one set of sheets for that bed. They needed to be washed, and she'd have to check for Jake's things in that room and guest bath. Thank goodness he hadn't moved more than a suitcase in yet. Any hint they were sleeping in separate bedrooms would be a sure giveaway that this was a marriage of convenience.

After saying a quick hello to Oliver, letting Daisy out of her training crate for a potty break and checking on the raccoons, she went into Jake's room. A change of clothes was folded on the foot of the bed. She stripped off the sheets and rushed them to the laundry room. Daisy happily scampered after her from room to room as if this was a new game, and she only tinkled on the floor once.

Jessica opened all the drawers in his room but only found a few things in and on the bedside table. In the guest bathroom, his shaving cream and toothbrush were on the counter. They were only a few simple things but they made it obvious they were not sharing a room.

She called Jake, but once again got voice mail. That's when she remembered he was teaching a safety class this afternoon and wouldn't be home until after five o'clock. She left a short message telling him her aunt would be here when he got home and then made another pass through the house.

Once everything was ready for a guest, she took Daisy outside to play and took her first deep breath. The house was ready, but was she?

And was it wrong to be excited about an overnight guest because it would allow her to openly show affection for her husband?

Chapter Nineteen

Who's here in a rental car?

Jake hadn't seen the small black car until he parked beside Jessica's SUV. His pulse jacked up a notch. He'd been in a rush this morning and carelessly left some of his things on the guest bathroom counter and clothes on his bed.

One step inside the front door, Jess wrapped her arms around his neck, and he automatically circled her waist in response.

"Welcome home, honey." She pressed her lips to his in a quick hello sort of kiss.

Her enthusiastic welcome was a surprise, but at the same time, he liked it too much for his own good. And it was a clear message that someone who could not know their secret was here. Which included everyone.

"Hey, sweetheart. How was your day?" he asked, understanding his cue to perform.

"It's been great. My aunt Kay has come for a visit."

He followed her gaze to the tall redheaded woman in the kitchen and returned her smile. He'd been so focused on Jess's surprising welcome home that he hadn't even seen her standing there.

Jess's aunt rushed forward and pulled them both into a back-patting hug. "It's so good to meet you."

"You, too," he said.

"I hope you don't mind me popping in like this?"

"Of course not." When Jessica started to walk away, he grasped her hand. "Family is always welcome, and I'm happy to finally meet some of my wife's."

"I tried to call you," Jess said.

"I had my phone on silent for the class." He pulled it from his pocket and saw her missed calls. "Sorry. I forgot to take it off Silent. I should go grab a shower and then I can come visit." He gave Jess a silent look that he hoped conveyed his question.

"Oh, I moved the lockbox for your gun from the bedside table to the top shelf of your side of the closet."

Thankfully, in a very short time they had developed a way of communicating that usually took years, and she understood his questioning glance.

"If you ladies will excuse me." He almost laughed

when Jess tugged him toward her room, just in case he hadn't received her message.

With another quick kiss on her pretty lips—for added effect *and* his pleasure—he veered right instead of left….and went into the master bedroom. That's when it hit him.

We'll be sharing a bed. For how long?

The large space suited Jessica, with lots of color and warmth. But now, some spare change and the dressy watch he'd worn for their wedding were on one of the bedside tables. Her side had a candle, a few photographs and loose jewelry. The clothes he'd left tossed on his bed were hanging in the closet where her scent filled his lungs. His things from the guest bathroom were mingled with hers. His shaving cream sat beside her bottles of lotion.

While her aunt was here, they'd be living like a real married couple. Almost.

After dinner and telling stories about Jess as a child, Kay said good night and went to bed, leaving them all alone with half a bottle of wine and rain softly tapping the windows.

"Let's take this and go into the bedroom so we can talk," she whispered.

"Good idea."

She set the bottle on her bedside table. "I'm so sorry this got sprung on you."

"No worries." After one more sip, he put their glasses beside the bottle. "I'd say it's going pretty good."

"I think so, too. I'll be back in a few minutes." She went into the bathroom.

He wanted to tell her about his new job offer, but now didn't seem like the right time. Not while her aunt was visiting. Jake changed into pajama bottoms, then paced the dark bedroom, but he got into bed when the shower turned off. Every second he waited, the rain grew heavier, pelting the metal roof in time with his heartbeat.

The bathroom door swung open, and light spilled out with honeysuckle-scented steam, along with the most seductive woman he'd ever seen. She was wearing the same unicorn pajamas as the day he'd caught her baking, but this time, she would be beside him.

In bed.

At the exact moment she turned off the bathroom light, thunder cracked, and the room lit up like midday. Jess yelped and leaped onto the bed as if the floor had turned to lava. Another flash of light caught her midair, right before her landing.

The bed bounced, and he was laughing so hard he couldn't talk for a few seconds.

"Oh my God. That scared the pants off me," she said between giggles.

The puppy whimpered in her crate for a second, then was silent.

"I can't believe she slept through that," he said.

"Good thing Loki and Floki's kennel is in the kitchen because they are probably awake and chattering away."

They rolled to face one another, and her smile

and eyes were bright with laughter. "So how was your day, wife?"

Raising her hand, she let it hover in the air between them, but instead of touching him, she rested it on the mattress a few inches from his. "That lightning strike was the second time today I've had a panic attack. My aunt's call was the first. I'm sorry her visit got sprung on you like this. I only found out a few hours before she got here."

"It's okay. I had a surprise visitor today, too."

"Who?" The rain had grown louder on the metal roof, and they moved closer to hear one another.

"My mother."

Jess grasped his hand. "No! Did she find out before you called her?"

"Yep."

"Was it terrible? Does she hate me? Is she mad?"

"No." *Liar.* "She just needs a little time to adjust to the news." Turning his hand over, he laced their fingers. "This charade is tougher than I thought."

"What's the toughest part for you?"

"Want the honest answer?"

"Yes, please." Her voice was soft as a kitten.

He brought their joined hands to his lips and kissed the back of hers. "Resisting you is the hardest part."

Her breath caught. "For real? Me, too."

A weight lifted from his mind. "What should we do about this?"

Please say take off our clothes.

"What *should* we do or what do we *want* to do?" she asked, then brushed her foot against his.

He wanted so much more than sex. Jake wanted to make love to her. Something shifted in the area of his guarded heart.

At the same moment, they moved toward one another, her lips so temptingly close. He brushed the back of his knuckles across her cheek. "For me, the *want* is screaming the loudest." Louder than the rain and thunder. Louder than his sensible side that kept yelling caution. But he didn't care about consequences when she was warm and willing, her hand trailing a teasing path across his bare chest.

"It will be easier to play our roles if we aren't trying to fake intimacy."

"Excellent point, sweetheart." He crushed his lips to hers. The kiss pulled them both into a new stage of life, and he didn't want to look back. Stroking his tongue against hers, he told her with every caress just how amazing she was.

Jess's eager response ramped up an experience he'd never forget, because it was new and wonderful and like no other. Soft skin yielded under his mouth and hands as he explored the curve of her back. He took in the taste of her, the emotion and the desire reflected in her eyes.

He couldn't remember feeling this way the first time he got married. The time that was supposed to be a real marriage, yet never really was. Back then, he hadn't even known what it truly was to love a woman. But now, wrapped around Jess, he was feeling things that were new and scary and kind of amazing.

While thunder rolled across the night sky, they made love, then slept wrapped around one another.

The next morning, Jessica woke draped across Jake's bare chest and the sensations of last night's fireworks and glitter made her body tingle all over again. Waking in their honeymoon suite had been amazing, especially when Jake had held her and run his fingers through her hair. But this bright sunshiny morning was…the best.

This time, they were skin to skin, and no one was pulling away.

"How'd you sleep, sweetheart?" he asked.

His gravelly morning voice vibrated under her ear and sent delicious shivers through her body. She raised herself to look at him, so handsome with tousled hair and stubble accentuating his bone structure. "I slept great. Don't freak out, but Oliver is sleeping beside your leg."

He glanced down without moving. "And I'm still alive. Guess he's not the wildest cat in *this* house."

He surprised her when he rolled her onto her back and looked at her with molten blue eyes. Her body was already addicted to his and the way he could make every muscle quiver with something brand new and wonderful. "Who's wild? You or me?" She wrapped her legs around him.

"You are wild and wonderful and so sexy." His

lips hovered above hers. "And the most amazing lover."

His words washed over her and began healing a wound left by another. This man, her husband, was the piece she hadn't known was missing.

Once they forced themselves from bed, they dressed and had breakfast with Aunt Kay.

While her aunt was on the phone, Jake pulled Jess aside. "I think I should probably go over to my house and talk to my mom. I only had a few minutes with her yesterday."

"Do you want me to go with you?" She really didn't want to, but she would if he needed her.

"You stay here with your aunt and visit. I won't be gone long."

A snap of cold caught her by surprise. The thought of his being gone for even an hour made her ache. How was she going to deal with his leaving for Dallas? "You'll call me if you need me?"

"Yes."

She kissed her husband goodbye at the front door, then turned to see her aunt grinning from ear to ear.

"You two are the cutest."

"You think so?"

"Absolutely. I already approved the money you requested, and it should be in your account. What are you going to do with it?"

Jessica sat across from her aunt at the table. "I'm going to build my clinic and hire a couple of employees for when there are a lot of animals here at the wildlife rescue."

"Sounds like you've really given it some thought. That's good. Seeing you happy and in love makes what I did worth fudging the truth."

"The truth? Worth it?" Pressure built inside her. "What did you do?"

Aunt Kay wore an I've-been-caught expression. "Um. Nothing. Never mind me. What should we do now?"

"Aunt Kay. Tell me what you did."

"Well… I might've fudged the part about you needing to be married."

Jessica almost choked on her sip of coffee and coughed hard enough to bring tears to her eyes. "Are you kidding me? You mean there's nothing in the trust fund about marriage?"

"Well…" Kay wrung her hands, then looked up with a sheepish smile. "Technically, no. But aren't you glad I did it? If I hadn't, you probably wouldn't have put yourself out there and fallen in love."

Jessica's pulse hammered in her temples. Little did her aunt know that fudging the truth was going to leave Jessica crying in her pillow and not living in happily-ever-after land once Jake left Oak Hollow.

She'd been upset with her dead father, and instead of finding a final resting place for his ashes, she'd put the urn on a shelf. She'd been blaming the need for their charade on him, but it was her aunt who deserved the blame.

"You're awfully quiet," Kay said. "Are you terribly mad at me?"

Jessica met her gaze. "I've been mad at my father."

"Oh, honey." Kay reached across the table and patted her arm. "I'm sorry. I should've just talked to you about this. When your father was in the hospital after...he was shot. He made me promise to do everything I could to encourage you to open your heart and find love."

If Jake found out, would he think she'd tricked him? Jessica didn't know who to be most upset with.

How about myself?

Chapter Twenty

Even though Pops had been the one who called and told his mother about his elopement, Jake owed him thanks for keeping her from coming out to the ranch. Things needed to be talked over and smoothed out before Jessica was in the same room with his mother.

The melody of an old-school country song played loud enough to be heard on the front porch, and when he walked into the living room, he was hit with long-ago childhood memories he'd almost forgotten were real. His parents were dancing. In the middle of the room, holding one another close, and dancing in a way divorced people did not.

Thank God I didn't catch them— He didn't even want to finish that thought.

"Am I interrupting?"

Their startled expressions almost made him laugh.

"Nope," Pops said and crossed the room to turn down the music. "Just a song we both like to dance to."

His mother smoothed her shirt and hair, then sat on the couch. "Let's talk."

"I'm sorry I didn't call you right away." Jake sat on the other end of the couch. "It happened fast and—"

"Fast?" Her voice shot out like a slap. "More like a lightning strike that blows something up. You barely know her and—"

"Jewels." Pops cut her off. "We discussed this. Let the boy talk."

Jake flexed his fingers. "Sometimes you just know when it's the right thing to do." He was not looking forward to hearing *I told you so*. It would be so much easier if he could tell them the truth, but he couldn't. He'd promised Jessica he'd keep their secret. Forever. "And I did know her as a teenager."

"Jessica is an amazing woman," Pops said. "You should see the way she looks at Jake with so much love in her eyes."

She does? Warmth washed across his skin. Was Pops just saying that…or was it true?

His mother's sigh was long and dramatic and belonged on a soap opera. "I just can't understand why you'd make this rash decision right when you're on the brink of a career you've wanted since you were a kid."

"This has nothing to do with my career."

"Exactly," she said. "You weren't thinking about

what you've worked so hard for when you jumped into this marriage."

"You have no idea what I was thinking about." *Like saving the family home.*

"Jewels," Pops said. "Tell him where this is coming from."

She stared at her lap, then met Jake's eyes. "Did you know I wanted to be a professional dancer?"

"What? No."

"I had a chance to go to Chicago, but I fell in love and got married. I will never ever regret having you." She took her ex-husband's hand in hers. "But I let it put a strain on our marriage."

Now Jake saw where this story was going. "Because you wish you'd gone to Chicago?"

She waved her free hand. "The point is, I don't want you to have regrets later."

"I understand what you're saying."

"Our son can still have a career right here in Oak Hollow. I have no doubt he will talk them into adding a K9 unit at some point."

That's when Jake realized both of his parents believed he planned to stay in Oak Hollow. When he was about to set them straight about his plans, the words wouldn't come.

He had to think carefully before speaking. His mother was a pro at digging up information and he could not get tripped up and say something that would give away their secret. He also needed to take a long look at why he was hesitating to say he was going back to Dallas. And he needed to think about what his mother had said.

An hour later, he left with his mother only slightly less upset, but she had promised to give them space.

Jake sagged onto the couch beside Jess, exhausted from Aunt Kay's whirlwind visit and the stress of monitoring every word in front of her and his parents. She rested her head on his shoulder, and he stroked her hair, the feel of the silky strands reducing his stress. Even though they were alone with no curious eyes and ears, he had no desire to go back to separate bedrooms. And if the way she touched him was any indication, neither did his wife.

Suddenly, nothing about being her husband felt fake.

"I know my aunt can be a lot. Thanks for being so good about all this."

"No problem. My mother has me well trained for situations like this. Kay is a light breeze compared to Hurricane Jewels."

Circling his chest with her arm, she snuggled closer against his side. "We haven't had a chance to talk about your visit with your parents. How did it go when you went over there?"

"My mom has been staying with Pops since she got to town." He knew what Jess was asking, but he didn't want to go into their family discussion right now. "I think my parents might be… I'm not sure how to put it."

She tipped her head to look at him. "Do they suspect something?"

"No, they don't." Her pretty mouth was so close to his, he couldn't resist brushing his lips across hers, loving the way she sighed. "I was going to say, I suspect they are getting back together or dating or something."

"Really?" She popped into a sitting position. "How do you feel about that?"

"I'm not sure. They haven't been together since I was a teenager, so it's surprising. But I want them to be happy."

"Do you think they are? Happy to be together?"

"Seems so. I caught them dancing. And Pops has been calling her out on things that he used to ignore. She actually seems to be trying to think about what she says."

"That sounds like a good thing. Think she'll ever move back to Oak Hollow?"

"I hadn't even considered that. Maybe I'm just reading too much into it.".

"I can feel your tension. How about I give you that backrub I promised?"

Fire raced through his blood. "I'll take you up on that."

"Go take a hot shower so your muscles are relaxed. I need to put the horses in their stalls and check on the pregnant goat."

"If we split up the chores, we'll get it done faster. I'll take Daisy and tend to the horses. Part of her training is getting her used to being around them.

You can take care of the goats and raccoons." He chuckled and shook his head. "And these are things I never thought I'd say."

But he was enjoying every minute of being here.

Jessica finished her share of the evening chores, but Jake was working on some simple commands with Daisy in the front yard, so she jumped in the shower. Tonight, instead of cotton pajamas, she put on a red silk nightgown that fell past her knees with a deep V between her breasts. But with her hand on the bathroom door, she hesitated.

What if I go out there like this and he doesn't want more than last night?

Not trusting herself to be the best judge of what a guy was thinking, her safest bet would be to get a robe from her closet, but when she came out of the bathroom, Jake was standing in her bedroom with wet hair, no shirt and a very well-fitted pair of black boxer briefs.

Hit with a new kind of hunger, she was energized and weak at the same time. Last night they'd undressed in the dark, using their hands to explore with only occasional flashes of lightning illuminating his naked body. But seeing him in the bright light, he was wow times ten. Jake could make money as an underwear model, but she didn't want to share him with the world.

"You are so beautiful," he said.

"I was just thinking the same about you." The soft smile on his face and fire in his eyes gave her the confidence to walk proudly toward him. No man had ever looked at her this way or made her feel like she was enough. Until now. She took his outstretched hands and drew close for a kiss.

His warm mouth teased her lips, working his way along her neck, sliding a strap from her shoulder. He moaned before lifting her and carrying her to the bed. "We might not get any sleep tonight, sweetheart."

The special glittery feeling only he could kindle was spiking to an off-the-charts level. "I'm okay with that."

And later that night, without any need for discussion, they slept in the same room, snuggled together on one side of the bed.

Separate bedrooms were a thing of the past and town gossip about their sudden marriage had died down to a dull roar. Jake hadn't named a date for when he'd move back to Dallas, and she didn't dare ask. Then all she'd do was count down the days and miss out on enjoying the time they still had together. Every moment was a gift, and she'd do as many of the things she dreamed of doing for however long they had left.

The next couple of weeks were busy and exciting. Morning cuddles and coffee, meeting for lunch on the square and cooking together at night became a happy routine. They rode horses each evening or took long walks and made love until they fell asleep.

And she took comfort in the fact that Dallas was only a car or airplane trip away.

Work had begun on her veterinary clinic, and Jake had paid bills and made friends with Oliver. They added fencing to the area between her house and the river, so the horses and goats had a place to graze during the day. One evening they had dinner with his parents at the Acorn Café, and Jewels had been unusually quiet, but no one encouraged her to talk, fearing what she might say.

Today's activity was a romantic picnic. Jessica turned to get the fruit from the refrigerator but had to wait as a puppy, a cat and two raccoons scampered by. Smiling from ear to ear, she packed a picnic basket and prepared to surprise Jake with an outdoor dinner under Granddaddy Oak.

The raccoons were big enough that they needed to spend some time outside practicing their climbing skills. She put them into a second basket, and they headed out the front door. From the porch she could see Jake working under the tree. He was building the bench she'd asked for and now every time she sat there, she could picture him and relive some of the happiness of this moment.

Daisy's happy bark made Jake looked up from his work under the big oak. The puppy bounded toward him, followed by the other animals and their leader, Snow White. Jess had a blanket under her right arm, a picnic basket in one hand and a basket of raccoons in the other. Goats trotted beside her, and bringing up the rear, a big orange cat ambled along at his own pace. With the horses already grazing loose in the area, the whole menagerie was here.

He dropped the screwdriver into the toolbox and took in the sight of her. It was almost like a painting or movie. She was the prettiest thing he'd ever seen in a sundress and wide-brimmed hat. He smiled, remembering the day she'd worked on the fence in the ripped and stained baggy jeans. The same ones she'd worn on the roadside the day she'd arrived in town. Back then he'd thought they were awful, but while watching her work, he'd found them surprisingly sexy. Maybe it was because he knew what was underneath the faded denim.

"Everyone wanted to bring dinner to you," Jessica said.

"You're not kidding. The whole crew is with you." He kissed her in a way that felt so natural, then took the blanket and spread it on the ground in the shade of the big oak. Daisy grabbed one corner with her teeth and shook her head with a growl.

"Daisy, no." He gave her a chew toy Jess handed to him. "You're not worried the raccoons will run away?"

"They won't get too far. They know who has the food."

"Speaking of food, I'm starving." He sat on the blanket and rubbed Daisy's tummy. "What did you bring?"

"Food for the puppy and raccoons so they won't eat ours." She started taking everything out. "For us, bread from the bakery, meat, cheeses and fruit. And brownies."

"Homemade?"

"Yes."

"How come you haven't been baking as much as you used to?" He plucked a grape off the bunch and popped it into his mouth.

"Because I tend to bake more when I'm stressed or worried."

"You mean I have to upset you to get some cookies?"

"I could be convinced to do more happy baking." She leaned his way and wrapped her arms around his neck for a slow, deep kiss.

If they weren't outdoors in the daylight, he'd do something to make both of them happy.

Once they had eaten and shared a bottle of wine, most of the animals were curled up and sleeping. The puppy was by his side, and the cat and the baby raccoons snuggled together near Jess. Even the new baby goat was asleep at the edge of the blanket while her momma grazed nearby.

"Did you ever think this is what you'd be doing on your day off?"

"No. The puppy is the only thing I would've thought of." As he lay with his head in her lap, he kissed her stomach. He could so easily picture her belly round with his baby growing inside. A toddler or two playing under this tree. He grew suddenly light-headed.

Is that just a dream...or is it my *dream?*

Even though he'd started to bring of his job several times, Jake had not told anyone about the promotion he'd been offered, and he needed to think hard about why that was.

His mother's cautionary story about passing up her chance to be a dancer kept going through his mind. He and Jess had a plan to tell everyone they were going to stay married when he first moved to Dallas, but he wanted to stay married. For real. What if they actually lived the way they were going to tell everyone? Jess had said long-distance relationships never work, but it wasn't impossible. And after he got more experience with the Dallas K9 unit, he would find a way to talk Oak Hollow into adding one that he could head up, whether it was less pay or not.

But until then, Dallas wasn't that far away. Jenny McKnight drove there several times a month to the fashion house she designed for. Maybe they could carpool, or she and Jess could. They could find a way to keep seeing one another.

"What's wrong?" she asked and caressed his cheek.

"What makes you ask that?"

"Your jaw tenses when something is wrong."

"I just don't want this day to end." He couldn't seem to make himself say more. Not yet.

Late the next afternoon, Jake was having trouble focusing on anything. He'd been putting off calling Dallas, but while they waited for their dinner guests to arrive, he slipped out onto the porch and called

Captain Phillips. He needed to figure out what he was doing and let Anson and Jessica know.

"Hello. Glad you called, Jake."

"Oh, yeah? What's the news in Dallas?"

"Sullivan has officially announced he'll retire at the end of the month."

Jake's pulse faltered, then raced. "That's sooner than he first said."

"It is. Think you'll be able to come back in a couple of weeks? Your promotion is waiting. And everyone will be glad to have you back."

"I need to talk to my dad, and the Oak Hollow police department and my wife."

"Wife? What did I miss?"

He hadn't meant to say that last part, but now the news was out. "Did I forget to mention that I got married?"

"Yes, you did. Congratulations. Is this why you seem hesitant?"

"I've just got more things to consider now. I'll talk to everyone and get back to you soon."

"Good deal. I gotta go, but we'll talk soon."

He put his phone in his pocket and turned to see Jess moving around inside getting things ready for their guests. He couldn't hear what she was saying but could see her talking to one of the animals. How was it possible to feel both joy and sadness at the same time?

Positions on this K9 squad didn't come along every day. He'd worked his butt off for years to become a team member they wanted. This was his chance. The chance he'd prayed for. And likely his only shot for a long time.

But is that still my biggest dream?

When Anson and Tess drove up, he shoved this issue momentarily aside and went to greet them.

Standing at the barbecue grill with Anson, he told him about his phone call to Dallas.

His friend's face crumpled into a confused frown. "You're still thinking about going back to Dallas?"

Jake shrugged. "It's a possibility."

"I thought since you got married and Jessica is starting her practice that we'd get to keep you here."

"It would not only be a promotion but also a position on First Squad. That's something that doesn't come along very often."

"Hmm. And it is what you've always talked about and wanted." Anson rubbed his beard. "What does your wife have to say about it?"

"She knew it was a possibility before we got married."

"And she married you knowing you might leave Oak Hollow?" His expression showed surprise.

"She did." What he couldn't say was, she'd married him so they could both have the careers they wanted. In different cities. "I haven't had a chance to tell her about my phone call yet." They turned at the sound of another car coming down the gravel driveway. "Let's table this conversation for later." But he couldn't put this off much longer.

Chapter Twenty-One

Jessica sat at the dining table with Tess, Jenny and Alexandra, who looked like she was ready to give birth at any moment.

"My doctor says four more weeks, but I have a feeling it might be sooner. This little lady is a mover."

When Jessica put a glass of lemonade in front of Alexandra, the mom-to-be pulled her free hand to her belly. "Feel that."

Jessica's throat grew thick with an overwhelming surge of maternal longing. "You're not kidding. She's doing gymnastics in there."

This made the other women come over to share the joy. While they laughed and talked, Jessica opened a bottle of white wine while glancing at Jake through the sliding glass door. The guys were laughing now, but earlier, he and Anson's expressions had grown serious and something about it made her chest tighten. But she didn't have time to analyze that right now.

Jessica poured a glass of wine and held it out to Tess.

"No wine for me," Tess said, then ducked her head with a smile she tried to hide.

Alexandra gasped. "Are you pregnant?" She said it loudly, right as the guys came in through the sliding glass door.

"Who else is pregnant?" Luke asked.

"Sorry." Alexandra mouthed to Tess, then bit her thumbnail.

All male eyes snapped to their spouses. Jake's eyes widened and flicked back and forth from Jessica's face and belly. She couldn't get a good read on his expression. There was some degree of bewilderment, but also something else. Something tender and… Could it be hope?

Tess's full-dimpled smile was big and bright as she took her husband's hands, but Anson's face was completely neutral, as if he was too afraid to even hope.

"I was going to wait until tonight, but I can't. Surprise, honey. We're having a baby."

Anson's expression morphed into pure joy. Better than a kid on Christmas morning. He kissed her, then dropped to his knees and pressed his cheek against her still flat stomach.

There was laughter, words of congratulations and even a few tears.

"I think he's happy," Luke said as he massaged Alexandra's shoulders. "Who's going to be next? Jenny or Jessica?"

Eric hugged his wife. "I hope it's us."

Jessica glanced at Jake, wishing he'd come say the same thing to her. In this joyous moment, she was hit with an ache she'd never experienced. It started in her core, and within seconds worked its way to her heart.

I'd love to have Jake's baby.

When their eyes connected, he crossed the room and drew her into a hug so tight their heartbeats raced together.

The following day, a car pulled up in front of her cabin, but Jessica could tell by the sound that it wasn't Jake's truck. When she looked out the window, she gasped and cursed as her lungs constricted. Jewels Carter was headed for her front door, and Jake wasn't home to give her backup. Whatever the reason for this drop-in visit, she was as nervous as Jake would be shut in a room full of cats.

With her brightest smile in place, she answered the door. "Hello. I'm so glad you've come to visit. Please come inside."

"Thank you." Jewels swept inside with the scent of floral perfume and assessed the room. "You have a beautiful home."

"Thank you. I do love it. Can I get you a drink?"

"No, thanks. Do you have time for a chat?"

"I sure do. Let's sit." Jessica tucked her hands under her arms so his mother wouldn't see them tremble. "I guess you're back in town for tomorrow's Founder's Day picnic? Jake is excited to introduce the new mounted division."

Jewels laced her fingers and twirled her thumbs around one another. "I'm here to support my son and make sure he doesn't make a mistake. Oak Hollow has chosen to spend money on the horses instead of a K9 unit. Not what my son wants to do with his life. Since he was a little boy, he's always wanted to work with dogs, not horses."

Jessica's stomach twisted into a tight, constricting knot. "I know. He's told me all about it."

"Are you prepared to sell your ranch and move to Dallas so he can follow *his* dream?"

"I…" Jessica's throat knotted much like her stomach. She wasn't at all prepared for this visit, especially being alone with her. Not to mentioned she'd worked herself into a frenzy just thinking about the next time she saw Jake's mother.

"I can see by the look on your face that you are not planning to move, and I can understand that. I'm sure you've worked very hard to have this ranch and start your own veterinary practice. But do you realize you're holding Jake back from a career he's also worked very hard for? A career he's wanted for a very long time."

"I don't want to hold him back." Her throat was painfully tight.

"But you are. He's sacrificing his wants and needs for you, and someday that will ruin your marriage. There will come a point when he'll resent you for it."

Has Jake decided to stay in Oak Hollow and just not told me yet?

Her eyes stung as she blinked back tears, and she was too afraid to hope. "I want him to be happy. I love him." This was the first time she'd said it aloud and the truth of it stole her breath.

"I'm not trying to be mean, but I have to look out for my son when no one else will. Now that he's been offered an even bigger promotion, that's more of a reason for him to come back to Dallas. But he told his captain that he hadn't made a final decision yet. He said he might have to stay here because you need him."

The words struck her like lightning. *Need him?* She wanted him with all her heart, but she didn't *need* him to take care of her. And why hadn't he told her about a bigger promotion?

Jewels stood and tugged on the hem of her pale-blue linen shirt. "I've taken up enough of your time, and I'm sorry if I've upset you. I just couldn't sit back and watch my son make a huge mistake that he'll surely regret." One foot out the door, she looked over her shoulder. "If you really love him, talk to him and help him see what's the right thing to do."

"I will." She could barely get the words out.

"Good. I'll see you tomorrow at the picnic."

The second Jewels drove away, silent tears streamed down her face. She'd been selfishly hoping he'd change his mind about going back to Dallas, and it sounded like he might be considering it. But this visit from his mother was a wakeup call. This whole marriage of convenience had been her idea. She had been a self-centered spoiled brat to put Jake in this situation, and she could not hold him back. That hadn't been part of the deal. He'd helped her fulfill her career dream, and she had to do the same for him.

She went to her bedside table drawer and pulled out their Recipe for a Fake Marriage. There might still be two question marks beside the words *End date*, but it was still part of the plan. This arrangement was always meant to come to an end.

The only right thing was to tell the man she loved it was time to end their charade.

When Jake got home an hour later, she was in bed with the shades drawn. He called her name, but she didn't answer. She listened to him moving around and greeting their pets, then a minute later, he came into their room and sat on the edge of the bed.

"Hey, sweetheart. Are you sick?"

"Just a bad headache. One of those where light and loud sounds hurt. But I took migraine medicine and should be all right after a good night's sleep." But she wouldn't be all right. Not when she had no choice but to send Jake to Dallas.

He stroked her hair back and kissed her forehead. "Can I get you anything? A drink?"

"Water would be good."

And a rewind button so I can go back and not break my own heart with lousy ideas.

"I brought home the department's trailer, and we need to have the horses in town by eight in the morning. Do you think you'll be okay to go?"

"I should be fine by morning."

When he came to bed a few hours later, she pretended to be asleep, but she let him hold her. Because it might be the last time. She knew what she had to do, but she needed a moment to get there. If he stayed, it might only be out of a sense of obligation, and she didn't want to be someone's obligation.

She wanted to be the love of someone's life.

The Founder's Day parade, led by Jake and two other officers on horseback, had been a success and now everyone was gathered near the gazebo for speeches and awards.

"What's wrong?" Emma asked Jessica.

"Nothing. I just have a headache today." This morning it was actually the truth. Her silent crying and a sleepless night had seen to that. She couldn't even stomach any of the delicious food. Fanning herself, she wiped sweat from her forehead.

"Are you sure it's nothing more?" Emma asked with a concerned look.

Jessica thought she was doing a pretty good job of hiding her pain, both mental and physical, but apparently not. "I'll be okay."

All the police officers and firefighters were lined up on each side of the gazebo. Jake looked so handsome in his dress uniform, and she wanted to start crying all over again.

Mrs. Jenkins, today's emcee—and the Oak Hollow resident who could outtalk anyone—continued to drone on and on. Whoever thought it was a good idea to give her the microphone was certainly learning their lesson along with the rest of them. "Who chose her to do the talking?" Jess asked under her breath.

"She probably chose herself," Emma whispered back. "And it doesn't hurt that her husband is on the city council."

"And now for our final award," Mrs. Jenkins said. "For bringing back the mounted division and celebrating our town's history, I'm happy to present this award to Officer Jake Carter."

Jessica's smile was the first real one of the day. She was so proud of the handsome man who looked cute and uncomfortable, and while the town cheered for him, she took photos.

Jake accepted the plaque, but Mrs. Jenkins wasn't ready to hand over the microphone.

"Officer Carter is always ready to do his job with a smile. I've watched Jake grow up, go off into the world and then come home when his family needed him. I'm real proud of this young man. Some of us thought we'd never find him a match and get him married, but he sure surprised us. Or maybe he just wanted to get us off his back," she said with a boisterous laugh, and much of the crowd chuckled along with her.

Jessica's nerves rattled. The topic of their marriage being discussed in such a public forum made her extra edgy. This woman just needed to give Jake the microphone and stop talking about her marriage.

But Mrs. Jenkins continued in her long-winded way. "Guess he didn't want to let her get away. He's smarter than I gave him credit for."

Jake leaned in toward the microphone. "Thank you so much for this award. It's an honor and easy to serve when you love your hometown." With Daisy on her leash, Jake returned to his spot with the other officers.

"Let's give him another hand," said Mrs. Jenkins. "I had my doubts, but I'm so happy to see that these two have been able to turn their marriage into a real one."

Jessica's head jerked back as if someone had slapped her.

No-o-o! This can't be happening!

Everyone was looking either at her or Jake. Her vision wavered, and she grabbed onto Emma's arm. "Get me out of here," she whispered. "Now."

"Are you going to be sick?"

"Yes." She was going to pass out or throw up, or maybe both. Thankfully they were right in front of Emma's shop, and with her friend supporting her, they quickly rushed inside.

She hurried into the bathroom and locked the door before splashing water on her face.

"Jess, where are you?" Jake called out. Alarm was evident in the tone of his voice.

"She's back here," Emma said.

Jake and Emma talked in hushed tones before one of them knocked on the door.

"Sweetheart, are you all right?"

Hell, no! This is a nightmare. "I'll be fine. I think the heat just got to me."

"Will you let me in, please?"

"Just give me a minute." She put down the toilet lid and sat with her head between her knees until the dizziness eased.

It had happened again. Public humiliation. And this time it was in a small town where she planned to stay and build a life with people she'd grown to love. How had their secret gotten out? Had Jake told someone? Had she slipped up and said something that tipped someone off?

However it had happened, she was paying the price for her ridiculous plan in a big way.

Chapter Twenty-Two

Standing in the middle of racks of women's clothing, Jake struggled as his heart tried to escape from a chest that was caving in.

"What the hell was Mrs. Jenkins talking about?" Emma asked.

"I..." He shook his head. The words wouldn't come.

Emma squeezed his arm. "I'll leave y'all to talk."

"Thanks." Daisy yipped and pulled on her leash, so he picked her up and cuddled her against his racing heart.

Why is this happening? How did our secret get out?

A couple of minutes later Jessica came out of the bathroom. "I just want to go home, please."

"I'll take you home and then come back for the horses."

He reached out to support her with an arm around her waist, but she rushed ahead of him out the back door of the shop, practically running to his truck parked on a side street. With Daisy tucked in the crook of one arm, he kept pace and then put the puppy in her car crate. Cranking up the AC as high as it would go, he pulled away from the curb.

"Talk to me, Jess."

"Not right now, please. I need a few minutes."

He was nauseous and every muscle was painfully stiff. The roar of the engine was the only sound and he was about to crawl out of his skin. There was nothing to do but think and get in his head. Had he unintentionally given away their secret? If so, he didn't know when or where. He glanced her way, but her expression was hidden as she curled her body toward the side window.

In front of their house, he put the truck in Park. "I'll tend to the animals in the barn once I get back with the horses. You can get some rest."

"Thanks." She got out and walked away without looking back.

Her mood was due to more than what had happened at the picnic or not feeling well. Something had been off with Jess since he'd come home last night, and he suspected it was more than a headache. Especially when he'd woken this morning and instantly sensed something was wrong. The spot beside him had been cold, the air thick with tension, and Jess had been in the kitchen with red eyes and no sign of her usual smile.

Could it be she'd fallen in love like he had and was upset about his leaving? If so, that was a problem they could work on together.

Another possibility slammed into his brain, and he cursed under his breath. If he hadn't told anyone... Had *she* told their secret? Was this guilt he was seeing?

The horses and goats were fed and in for the night, and now it was time to get his wife to talk to him. Walking in the front door, he was not met with anger or crying or her pretty smile. Jess wore a blank, eyes-glazed expression.

"Sorry," she said. "I had a momentary freak-out."

"I get that." He sat beside her on the couch and wanted to take her hand or hold her, but her crossed arms and stiff posture were not welcoming. "I'm freaking out, too. Please tell me what's going through your mind."

"Have you found a place to live in Dallas?"

"No." Maybe this really was about her not wanting him to leave. Even though he hadn't announced anything, he knew in his heart that he was planning to stay in Oak Hollow.

"You should probably do that. I know you don't want to live with your mother."

"What if I don't go back to Dallas?"

She inhaled a shaky breath. "You have to go. It's part of the plan. You helped me get what I wanted and now it's your turn."

Alarm rippled through him with a painful grip

around his torso. This is not what he'd thought she'd say. She finally looked at him full on, but her eyes were emotionless, and it nearly gutted him.

"Pops is doing great and I'm here to check in on him, and your promotion is waiting. It's time. We've found our end date, and it's now. A clean break is probably better than dragging it out."

"That's what you want? Really?" His voice was gruff from a throat tight and burning with the threat of unmanly tears.

She wrapped her arms around herself. "Yes. I'll always cherish our time together, and I'll be forever grateful."

"Grateful?" *Are you kidding me?*

"It's time we both got back to real life." Her voice cracked, and she cleared her throat. "Separate lives."

Her words rammed him square in the chest. "Jess? Why are you doing this? We talked about at least trying a long-distance relationship."

"We can still tell people that if you want. My clinic is being built, your bills are paid, you get your promotion and everybody wins."

Nothing about this felt like a win. Nothing. Not even the reality of his dream job.

"You've always known that I never planned to stay married to a man in a dangerous profession. I put the rest of the agreed-upon money in your account last night. And there is absolutely no rush to pay any of it back."

What in the ever-loving hell? Thank you for your

service, now take your money and leave? Had she left an extra fifty on his bedside table?

"The secret coming out like it did…" She kept talking as if his world wasn't shattering. "It's almost like we staged the whole thing."

His jaw dropped and his teeth clicked painfully when he snapped it closed. Had *she* staged it and that's why she'd been weird since last night? Now that he thought about it, she hadn't once asked him if he had told anyone.

"I'm going to take a long bath and see if I can get my headache to go away." She attempted a smile, but it wobbled. "You're a good man, Jake. One of the best I've ever known." Pushing herself up from the couch, she left him sitting there.

This is what happens when I open my heart for the first time in years?

The cat hopped up beside him and Jake didn't even flinch. Oliver could claw him to pieces, and it wouldn't hurt as bad as what he was already experiencing. Jake felt dismissed, as if he'd served his purpose, but he didn't know where to go. There would be too many questions from both of his parents if he went home. He'd already declined several of their calls as well as those from a few friends. He scratched the cat's head and glanced toward their room where he could hear the water running.

Maybe I just don't know her as well as I thought.

He shook his head. No. None of this was the behavior he'd grown to expect from her. Something was very off, and he could not just run off to Dallas without investigating this whole situation. Crushed and confused he got up to leave and go somewhere he could be alone, but when Jessica's phone rang from the coffee table with a ringtone he recognized as Aunt Kay's, for some reason he felt the need to answer the call. He was upset with Jess, but also worried.

"Hi, Kay. It's Jake."

"I can tell by your cute accent that it's you. But I can also tell you sound upset. What's wrong?"

"Does Jess get migraines very often?"

"No, maybe one or two a year. Is she all right? Do I need to come?"

"No, no. I think she'll be okay. She's taking a bath. She hasn't felt good since last night and… She's just not herself."

"Aren't you a sweet husband to be so worried about her."

"I love her." Unable to sit still, he walked to the windows and stared out at the ranch and home he'd grown to love. The tree where they'd picnicked.

"That's so wonderful to hear. I'm happy you're there to take care of her when I can't be. Is she still mad at me about the trust fund thing?"

The question confused him. "Mad at you? I don't think so."

"Even though Jessica didn't actually have to be married to get the money, I'm so glad she married you."

Jake stumbled like someone had kicked the back of his knees. "I need to go. She's calling for me."

"Okay. Call me back if you need me. Bye, dear."

I've been tricked into marriage. Again!

But why? None of this made any sense. Why would Jessica do this?

Chapter Twenty-Three

Ghostly shadows of tree branches danced across her ceiling and the wind battered raindrops against the windows. Jessica laid awake, her insides feeling much like the storm that had kicked up around midnight. Her tears had finally dried, leaving her numb and exhausted. Oliver was curled up on Jake's pillow, and the raccoons were chattering in their kennel, but the house was so quiet without Jake and Daisy. So empty.

She had her ranch. Her veterinary practice. Her money. But the price had been steeper than she'd bargained on, and now she had a broken heart. The last little piece had crumbled when she'd stood at the bedroom window and watched him drive away.

Why did I hide in the bathroom like a child?

But she knew why. If she'd come out to say good-bye, she would've begged him to stay in Oak Hollow. She would've taken back her suggestion that they needed to make a clean break. And that's not what was best for him.

"Ugh. I'm never going to get any sleep." Taking out her frustration with a karate kick to the covers, she dragged herself to the living room and paused by the urn holding her father's ashes. "You and your sister got me into this mess. Now what? If you have any ideas, maybe you could send me a sign?"

But she couldn't blame her father and aunt. She was the one who fell head over heels in love with a man she'd known would be leaving her.

Hopefully, once she was past the worst of her heartache, she'd see that this gut-wrenching decision had been for the best. No man had ever stayed in love with her for very long—if anyone ever really was to begin with. She'd been a stepping-stone on her ex-boyfriend's way to a woman he could marry. And she'd been what Jake had needed to take care of his family and further his career. Even though her decision was painful as hell, it was better that they parted now instead of dragging it on and falling deeper in love only to have him resent her later.

Over the next week, Jessica stayed busy on her ranch, working long hours until she was exhausted enough to sleep. She hadn't even told Aunt Kay what happened because she knew her aunt would come, and she didn't want to see anyone right now. Friends who knew the truth kept calling, and she continued to ask them for time alone and space to think.

But when Emma showed up at her house, she cried on her friend's shoulder and told her everything. The confusion about her trust fund. The fake marriage charade. Falling in love. Telling her story was cathartic, and it made her reflect and consider her future.

At the awards ceremony, she'd been triggered by a past she'd held on to for far too long. But no more. There was always going to be someone who talked about you or thought badly of you. The important thing was what those you loved thought. Losing Jake was a million times worse than any public embarrassment.

She loved him and didn't want to live the rest of her life regretting and wondering what they could've become. She wanted Jake Carter to be in her life, even if it was only part-time.

After the horrible, selfish way she'd ended things, was it too late to see if he would consider a long-distance relationship? Dallas was only six hours away, nothing compared to what military families went through. Missing someone between visits was better than pining for a love you'd lost.

Jake had hidden himself away after their breakup, once again the main topic of gossip in his hometown. Poor Jake had been fooled again. Another marriage down the toilet. And once again, he was running off to Dallas.

He shoved another moving box into the bed of his truck as Emma walked up the driveway.

"Hey, Emma."

"Hi. I'm glad I caught you before you left for Dallas."

"I've already been up there, and I'm just back for my stuff."

"Do you have a minute to talk?"

"Sure." He motioned for her to follow him to the backyard, and they sat on the patio chairs.

"I'm not one for meddling, but I also have some experience…" She took a measured breath. "Experience I wouldn't wish on anyone. I'm going to break a friend's confidence and tell you something."

"I'm listening." He rubbed his damp palms against his blue jeans.

"Love and family are precious, and I'm still grieving my husband and daughter. Although it's not the same kind of grief, I see you and Jessica hurting."

"Emma, she tricked me into marrying her. She used me." *Just like my first wife.*

"That's not what happened. Her aunt tricked her, and she didn't find out until after you were married. She truly thought it was the only way."

His heart jolted like he'd touched a live wire. "Honestly?"

"I swear." She sat forward in her chair. "Do you love her?"

"Yes. I really do and that's why I'm so…" He motioned to himself like the pain was a physical thing she could see.

Her smile was encouraging. "I'm going to tell you a few other things she confided. She pushed you away, even when it was breaking her own heart, because she doesn't want to keep you from your dream job, just the same way she wouldn't want someone to keep her from hers."

"She really said that?" When hope tried to push through his adrenaline rush, he shoved it back down.

"Yes. She said she didn't want you to stay out of a sense of responsibility. She does not want to be someone's obligation. She wants to be the love of someone's life. She loves you, too. A lot."

The intense weight of heartache lifted, and he could breathe without fighting for every inhale. He knew exactly what to do. If she wanted a love of her life, she had one, because she was the love of his, and he intended to let her know.

"Thanks, Em." He surprised her with a hug. "I have a few things I need to do."

Jake abandoned his packing and drove straight over to see Mrs. Jenkins. His talk with Emma had made some things as clear as crystal, but he needed a few more answers before he talked to his wife. He needed as much of the truth as he could gather.

Mrs. Jenkins opened her front door and immediately drew him into an enthusiastic hug. "Jake, I must apologize. I'm so sorry about what I said at the awards ceremony. Sometimes my mouth gets going before my filter can engage." She hooked her arm around his, tugged him inside and through the house to her kitchen table.

"Tell me what's on your mind."

"What did you mean when you said turn our marriage into a real one?"

"Well, mostly because of what my cousin told me."

"Which is…?" If his fingers drummed any harder, he'd make dents in her tabletop.

"She owns the antique store where you bought your wedding rings, and it seems she overheard y'all talking about a fake marriage. But seeing you two together, it's obvious you've fallen in love for real."

Another wave of calm washed over him. Neither of them had told their secret, they'd just been careless about what they said in public. He'd been embarrassed and devastated about the public outing and the end of his marriage, but now he was past caring what anyone thought. He had a wife to win back and wounds to heal. It was time to set things right.

"Mrs. Jenkins, can I get you to help me out with a couple of things?"

"Name it," she said with a twinkle in her eyes.

"First, I need you to call your cousin. I need another ring."

With Daisy riding shotgun on the floorboard in her crate, Jake drove to the antique store between Oak Hollow and San Antonio. They still had the ring with the large aquamarine stone. The one that had made Jessica's eyes sparkle.

Their marriage was so much more than a temporary charade. It had always been more, from the moment they had kissed in front of the judge. The charade had been the two of them trying to convince themselves they could play this out, then end it and walk away as friends. It was time to put it all on the line, because if he didn't give it a shot, he'd be walking around with half a heart.

He'd gladly give up the job in Dallas if it meant spending his days and nights with Jess and their animals on the ranch. He'd train Daisy and maybe start a dog training business of his own. And with Mrs. Jenkins's help, both with fundraising and her sway with the city council, he'd get Oak Hollow to start a K9 unit at some point. Pops was in Oak Hollow, and he suspected that if he stayed, his mom might move back to be with both of them. He had a job and coworkers he loved right here in his hometown.

And Oak Hollow was where he could be with the woman he loved.

Jessica was done debating what to do. If he'd talk to her after her terrible breakup performance, she'd ask him if they could have a long-distance relationship. She got out her recipe box and pulled out a blank card. Under the row of cupcakes, she wrote a new title: Recipe for a Long-Distance Marriage. If things went as she hoped, they could write it together.

Afraid Jake wouldn't answer if she called, she sent a text message.

If you're still in town, can we talk? Please.

Jake's response came a minute later.

I'm already on my way.

Her body flooded with endorphins, and she grasped the edge of the counter. "Who knew weak-kneed was a real thing?" He was coming. Maybe they had a chance. She sent one more message.

Meet me at the river.

Jessica was standing on Turtle Island watching the last colors of sunset slip below the horizon when she heard Daisy barking.

The puppy came into view right before Jake. She wanted to run to him and fall into his arms, but they needed to talk first. Evening darkness hid his expression, and even at his brisk pace, it seemed to take forever for him to get close.

When Daisy reached the riverbank, Jessica reached across the small strip of water and picked her up. "Hello, darling girl. I missed you."

"Did you miss me, too?"

His voice was a song she wanted to hear forever. "Yes, I did. Very much."

He stepped out onto Turtle Island, and for a moment, the only sounds were the water and the pounding beat of her own heart.

Daisy yipped and wiggled. He took the puppy,

clipped on her leash and hooked the other end to his belt loop.

"Jake, I'm so sorry for the way I treated you. I didn't know how else to make sure you didn't pass up this opportunity."

"Sweetheart, I understand now why you did it."

"I have an idea for starting over with a new plan." She handed him the second recipe card. "If you are open to the idea, I'd like to write this together."

"Recipe for a Long-Distance Marriage," he read aloud, then grinned at her. "I have a better idea, let's change the word *long-distance* to the word *real*."

She gasped, but he brushed a fingertip over her lips before she could speak.

"Jess, I want a real marriage with you. The kind where we live in the same town and in the same house."

"But your promotion? Your dream?"

"Dreams change, Mystery Woman. I can start my own dog training business. And I know I can convince the city to start a K9 unit. I've employed a secret weapon."

"You have?"

"Yes." One corner of his mouth turned up in a grin. "Mrs. Jenkins has already started working on fundraisers and employing her sway with the city council."

Her fingers tingled with the need to touch him, so she placed her hand lightly on his chest, and he clasped it to his heart. "And this is really what you want? Not because you think I need you here to take care of me?"

"You are the most capable woman I've ever known. I'm hoping we can take care of each other, because I love you, and it feels so damn good to tell you."

Her smile was so wide her cheeks ached. "Hearing it is even better. I love you, too." She flung her arms around him, and like someone lost finding home, they kissed with all the emotions they'd been holding back.

They only stopped when Daisy wrapped them in her leash.

"Seems this little lady is trying to make sure we stay together." Jake untangled them and then dropped to one knee.

She thought he was going to pick up the puppy, but when he took her hand and looked up at her with a question in his eyes, her breath caught.

Is he about to propose?

"I had to take a drive this morning to get this." He pulled a small box from his pocket and opened it to reveal the aquamarine ring from the antique store.

"Oh, Jake. You remembered."

"You are the love of my life. I love everything about you. The way you stain my clothes. The way you fall down."

That made her laugh as she wiped away a tear.

"Your loving nature. For all the wonderful things that make you the kind of woman a man wants to marry again, and again. Jessica Talbot, I choose you.

Will you have me for real and for keeps this time? Will you marry me, again?"

"Yes. Absolutely yes." Both of their hands trembled as he slipped it on her finger, right beside her golden wedding band. He stood and Jessica cradled his face. "I'll do more than have you, Jake Carter. I'll marry you again. I started falling in love with you the moment you caught me as we fell into the bluebonnets on the roadside."

"Me, too, Mystery Woman. I think that's what they call love at first sight," he said. "This time I want all our friends and family with us. How soon can we renew our vows?"

His eagerness melted her heart. "As soon as the girls and Aunt Kay can help me plan something. Are you free in…" She tapped her chin. "Two months?"

"For you, yes." He held her close, tracing the length of her back. "And please don't ever try to set me free again."

"I won't. Once was enough of that. I'm in this for keeps."

Epilogue

Oak Hollow Herald
Community Announcements

The city of Oak Hollow is pleased to announce that Officer Jake Carter, Master Trainer, will head up the development of Oak Hollow's new K9 unit.

In the weeks leading up to the wedding, Aunt Kay buzzed around town getting everything organized for an outdoor wedding on the ranch. This time Jessica had all her girlfriends with her as she prepared for the special day. Everyone, including flower girls Hannah and Lilly, were with her when she had her final dress fitting with Jenny. The gorgeous dress was an off-the-shoulder design with a tea-length skirt of whisper pink silk under a layer of white chiffon.

Jewels was there, too. She had once again come out to the ranch to see Jessica, but this time, she apologized and cried. Two things she rarely did. She thanked Jessica for making her son so happy and hoped they could be friends.

On a lovely summer evening, Jake and Jessica's friends and family—and a few animals—gathered on their ranch. The old oak tree was decorated with white lights, surrounded by flowers and draped with swags of gossamer fabrics in white and whisper pink. A long white canopy covered the tables.

Jessica stood behind her bridesmaids while everyone took their places. She felt like a princess in her dress. A real wedding dress for a real wedding ceremony.

Hannah and Lilly wore their flower girl dresses, and Cody once again escorted them down the aisle to where Jake stood with Daisy by his feet and his friends lined up beside him.

Pops held out his arm for Jessica. "I'm real proud to walk you down the aisle. Are you ready?"

"I'm so ready," she said.

From the moment the music started, a sense of peace and joy filled Jessica. They said their vows using a lot of the same words they'd said when he proposed by the river and gave her a ring. The ceremony was short, and the reception was joyous. Food, drinks, music and dancing filled the night. But most of all, love filled everyone's hearts.

When Alexandra and Luke's baby girl started crying in her stroller, Jake picked her up and cradled her in the crook of one arm. "Don't cry, sweetie, this is a very happy day."

She stopped crying and gazed at him with big curious eyes.

Jessica leaned against her husband's shoulder and gazed at the precious baby girl. "And there you go, making another woman fall in love with you."

"Don't worry. You're my number one, sweetheart." He pulled a recipe card from his pocket. "This is for you."

She unfolded the card and read it aloud. "Recipe for a Real Marriage. Jake, Jessica, love and lots of animals." She laughed and kissed him. "I like our new plan so much better than the first one."

The sun was setting on a warm spring evening about a year after Jessica had moved to Oak Hollow. A family of deer were drinking at the edge of the river but darted into the trees upon their approach.

She hugged the urn containing her father's ashes against her chest. "I'm sorry it has taken me so long to get to this. But I think you understand." Removing the lid, she let the breeze carry his ashes across the rippling water and into the trees. "I love you, Dad. Thank you for guiding me to the love of my life." She set the urn down on Turtle Island and let out a long slow breath.

Jake wrapped his arms around her from behind and cradled her rounding belly. "If our baby is a boy, let's name him after your father."

"That's a wonderful idea." She turned in his arms and ran her fingers up the back of his neck and into his hair. "And what if we have a girl."

"What about Gladys Kravitz," he teased.

She laughed. "I think not."

"I sure do love you, Mrs. Carter."

"And I love you, Officer."

* * * * *

For more marriage of convenience romances, check out these other great books from Harlequin Special Edition:

The Most Eligible Cowboy
by Melissa Senate

Their Texas Christmas Gift
by Cathy Gillen Thacker

The Night That Changed Everything
by Helen Lacey

Available now wherever Harlequin Special Edition books and ebooks are sold!

#2899 CINDERELLA NEXT DOOR
The Fortunes of Texas: The Wedding Gift
by Nancy Robards Thompson

High school teacher and aspiring artist Ginny Sanders knows she is not Draper Fortune's type. Content to admire her fabulous and flirty new neighbor from a distance, she is stunned when he asks her out. Draper is charmed by the sensitive teacher, but when he learns why she doesn't date, he must decide if he can be the man she needs...

#2900 HEIR TO THE RANCH
Dawson Family Ranch • by Melissa Senate

The more Gavin Dawson shirks his new role, the more irate Lily Gold gets. The very pregnant single mom-to-be is determined to make her new boss see the value in his late father's legacy—her livelihood and her home depend on it! But Gavin's plan to ignore his inheritance and Lily—and his growing attraction to her—is proving to be impossible...

#2901 CAPTIVATED BY THE COWGIRL
Match Made in Haven • by Brenda Harlen

Devin Blake is a natural loner, but when rancher Claire Lamontagne makes the first move, he finds himself wondering if he's as content as he thought he was. Is Devin ready to trade his solitary life for a future with the cowgirl tempting him to take a chance on love?

#2902 MORE THAN A TEMPORARY FAMILY
Furever Yours • by Marie Ferrarella

A visit with family was just what Josie Whitaker needed to put her marriage behind her. Horseback-riding lessons were an added bonus. But her instructor, Declan Hoyt, is dealing with his moody teenage niece. The divorced single mom knows just how to help and offers to teach Declan a thing or two about parenting—never expecting a romance to spark with the younger rancher!

#2903 LAST CHANCE ON MOONLIGHT RIDGE
Top Dog Dude Ranch • by Catherine Mann

Their love wasn't in doubt, but fertility issues and money problems have left Hollie and Jacob O'Brien's marriage in shambles. So once the spring wedding season at their Tennessee mountain ranch is over, they'll part ways. Until Jacob is inspired to romance Hollie and her long-buried maternal instincts are revived by four orphaned children visiting the ranch. Will their future together be resurrected, too?

#2904 AN UNEXPECTED COWBOY
Sutton's Place • by Shannon Stacey

Lone-wolf cowboy Irish is no stranger to long, lonely nights. But somehow Mallory Sutton tugs on his heartstrings. The feisty single mom is struggling to balance it all—and challenging Irish's perception of what he has to offer. But will their unexpected connection keep Irish in town...or end in heartbreak for Mallory and her kids?

*Mariella Jacob was one of the world's premier bridal
designers. One viral PR disaster later, she's trying to
get her torpedoed career back on track in small-town
Magnolia, North Carolina. With a second-hand store
and a new business venture helping her friends turn the
Wildflower Inn into a wedding venue, Mariella is
finally putting at least one mistake behind her.
Until that mistake—in the glowering, handsome
form of Alex Ralsten—moves to Magnolia too…*

Read on for a sneak preview of
Wedding Season,
the next book in USA TODAY *bestselling author
Michelle Major's Carolina Girls series!*

"You still don't belong here." Mariella crossed her arms
over her chest, and Alex commanded himself not to notice
her body, perfect as it was.

"That makes two of us, and yet here we are."

"I was here first," she muttered. He'd heard the argument
before, but it didn't sway him.

"You're not running me off, Mariella. I needed a fresh
start, and this is the place I've picked for my home."

"My plan was to leave the past behind me. You are a
physical reminder of so many mistakes I've made."

"I can't say that upsets me too much," he lied. It didn't
make sense, but he hated that he made her so uncomfortable.
Hated even more that sometimes he'd purposely drive by

her shop to get a glimpse of her through the picture window. Talk about a glutton for punishment.

She let out a low growl. "You are an infuriating man. Stubborn and callous. I don't even know if you have a heart."

"Funny." He kept his voice steady even as memories flooded him, making his head pound. "That's the rationale Amber gave me for why she cheated with your fiancé. My lack of emotions pushed her into his arms. What was his excuse?"

She looked out at the street for nearly a minute, and Alex wondered if she was even going to answer. He followed her gaze to the park across the street, situated in the center of the town. There were kids at the playground and several families walking dogs on the path that circled the perimeter. Magnolia was the perfect place to raise a family.

If a person had the heart to be that kind of a man—the type who married the woman he loved and set out to be a good husband and father. Alex wasn't cut out for a family, but he liked it in the small coastal town just the same.

"I was too committed to my job," she said suddenly and so quietly he almost missed it.

"Ironic since it was your job that introduced him to Amber."

"Yeah." She made a face. "This is what I'm talking about, Alex. A past I don't want to revisit."

"Then stay away from me, Mariella," he advised. "Because I'm not going anywhere."

"Then maybe I will," she said and walked away.

Don't miss
Wedding Season *by Michelle Major,*
available May 2022 wherever
HQN books and ebooks are sold.

HQNBooks.com

PHMMEXP0322

Get 4 FREE REWARDS!

We'll send you 2 FREE Books <u>plus</u> 2 FREE Mystery Gifts.

FREE Value Over **$20**

Both the **Harlequin® Special Edition** and **Harlequin® Heartwarming™** series feature compelling novels filled with stories of love and strength where the bonds of friendship, family and community unite.

YES! Please send me 2 FREE novels from the Harlequin Special Edition or Harlequin Heartwarming series and my 2 FREE gifts (gifts are worth about $10 retail). After receiving them, if I don't wish to receive any more books, I can return the shipping statement marked "cancel." If I don't cancel, I will receive 6 brand-new Harlequin Special Edition books every month and be billed just $4.99 each in the U.S or $5.74 each in Canada, a savings of at least 17% off the cover price or 4 brand-new Harlequin Heartwarming Larger-Print books every month and be billed just $5.74 each in the U.S. or $6.24 each in Canada, a savings of at least 21% off the cover price. It's quite a bargain! Shipping and handling is just 50¢ per book in the U.S. and $1.25 per book in Canada.* I understand that accepting the 2 free books and gifts places me under no obligation to buy anything. I can always return a shipment and cancel at any time. The free books and gifts are mine to keep no matter what I decide.

Choose one: ☐ **Harlequin Special Edition** ☐ **Harlequin Heartwarming**
(235/335 HDN GNMP) **Larger-Print**
(161/361 HDN GNPZ)

Name (please print)

Address   Apt. #

City   State/Province   Zip/Postal Code

Email: Please check this box ☐ if you would like to receive newsletters and promotional emails from Harlequin Enterprises ULC and its affiliates. You can unsubscribe anytime.

Mail to the **Harlequin Reader Service:**
IN U.S.A.: P.O. Box 1341, Buffalo, NY 14240-8531
IN CANADA: P.O. Box 603, Fort Erie, Ontario L2A 5X3

Want to try 2 free books from another series! Call 1-800-873-8635 or visit www.ReaderService.com.

---

*Terms and prices subject to change without notice. Prices do not include sales taxes, which will be charged (if applicable) based on your state or country of residence. Canadian residents will be charged applicable taxes. Offer not valid in Quebec. This offer is limited to one order per household. Books received may not be as shown. Not valid for current subscribers to the Harlequin Special Edition or Harlequin Heartwarming series. All orders subject to approval. Credit or debit balances in a customer's account(s) may be offset by any other outstanding balance owed by or to the customer. Please allow 4 to 6 weeks for delivery. Offer available while quantities last.

Your Privacy—Your information is being collected by Harlequin Enterprises ULC, operating as Harlequin Reader Service. For a complete summary of the information we collect, how we use this information and to whom it is disclosed, please visit our privacy notice located at corporate.harlequin.com/privacy-notice. From time to time we may also exchange your personal information with reputable third parties. If you wish to opt out of this sharing of your personal information, please visit readerservice.com/consumerschoice or call 1-800-873-8635. **Notice to California Residents**—Under California law, you have specific rights to control and access your data. For more information on these rights and how to exercise them, visit corporate.harlequin.com/california-privacy.

HSEHW22

Love Harlequin romance?

DISCOVER.

Be the first to find out about promotions,
news and exclusive content!

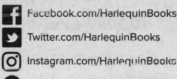

f Facebook.com/HarlequinBooks

▼ Twitter.com/HarlequinBooks

◎ Instagram.com/HarlequinBooks

℗ Pinterest.com/HarlequinBooks

You Tube YouTube.com/HarlequinBooks

ReaderService.com

EXPLORE.

Sign up for the Harlequin e-newsletter and
download a free book from any series at
TryHarlequin.com

CONNECT.

Join our Harlequin community to
share your thoughts and connect
with other romance readers!
Facebook.com/groups/HarlequinConnection

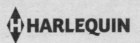

HARLEQUIN

Heartfelt or thrilling, passionate or uplifting—Harlequin is more than just happily-ever-after.

With twelve different series to choose from and new books available every month, you are sure to find stories that will move you, uplift you, inspire and delight you.